Full Circle

360°'s of Life

a novel by:
John W. Mangum

Full Circle
360°'s of Life

ISBN: 0-9840896-0-8

Cover photography by John Mangum

Running Iron Press
Novel edited & designed by Dan Grams
www.runningironpress.com

Dedicated to:
Miss Sassy Return, SI 98,
By Rocky Jones out of Light Return Jet

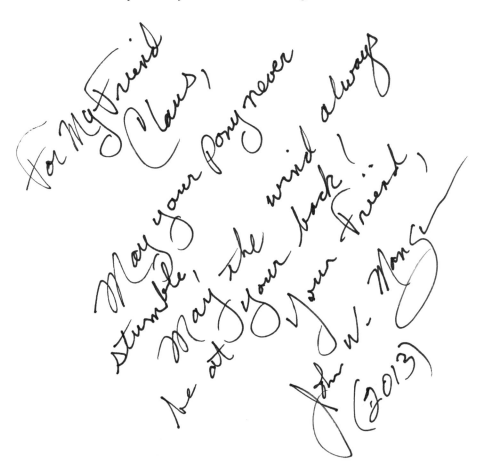

Chapter 1

Spring roundup was in full swing at the Blevins ranch. It had been the same tradition since the ranch was established shortly after the war for Southern Independence in 1865.

Granddad Levi Blevins, a strong willed, tight-jawed, old cowboy perched on his bay gelding at the top of a grassy knoll. It had been a long day and he felt it in his bones. He took off his sweat stained hat and wiped his face with his calico wild-rag. Below him the cattle he'd gathered were milling around grazing on dry grass.

As he gazed out over the vast open range he observed an old windmill squeaking as the fans slowly turned in the breeze. He made a mental note : *Gotta oil that damn thing one of these days.* His attention is diverted to a dust cloud to the West,a car speeding down the dirt road leading to the ranch headquarters. *Someone sure is in a hurry to get to the ranch.* About that time he heard cattle being herded towards him from the East.

Levi spun the bay around and spotted his two grandsons, Andy and Randy, and his lifelong sidekick Zeb Pike, driving what appeared to be about eighty-five head of cows and calves toward him. "Good work boys, several more days like this an we'll have this pasture branded as well as the Big Brushy."

Andy and Randy rode toward Levi continuing to drive the cattle toward those that Levi had gathered. "Yeah, Granddad, hopefully Randy can stay out here and help us."

Randy nodded. "I sure hope so. Being cooped up in town isn't my idea of living. The only excitement I have to look forward to is sports."

Curious who was stirring up the dust on the road into the ranch Levi turned back to the West. "Andy isn't that your Dad driving in here like a turpentined cat? He must think that damn dirt road is an interstate or somethin'."

"Yeah, that's him all right. He's probably mad because I didn't get back to town for school last Monday."

"He's had to brand before, surely he knows it's not just a weekend job."

"I know Andy, but he and Mom are pretty strict when it comes to missing school."

"I'll tell you boys one damn thing for sure when he was your age it didn't bother him to miss a little school when we had to brand. Hell, he'd just as soon miss school seven days a week."

Andy looked at Levi with a strange expression. "You know school only runs five days a week."

"School was seven days a week when I was your age. Seven days of blister popping work building fence and working cattle. You boys don't know what work is, Sometimes Dad made me carry a fifty-five gallon drum of water on my back to water cattle over in the Big Draw pasture."

The two boys looked at each other as though to say *has he been hittin' the jug or has the sun got to him.*

Zeb continued to bunch the cattle as he brought in the last of those he and the boys gathered. Levi, looked them over real close. "We had twice as many cattle as we do today when Samuel was your age. It took a couple of months to get 'em all branded. Now he's a doctor and doesn't want to have nothin' to do with the place. The only country he wants is that damn country club. If we had the dinero he and Verna spend there we could burn ours."

Levi's youngest son Jake rode up at a lope to meet up with the rest of the crew. "Been over to the Brushy. That damn pasture is rough as hell. Some of those arroyos have Mesquite so thick a man wouldn't have a stitch of clothin' on him if he tried to ride through it. I did manage to count about a hundred an twenty-five head of cows and calves and I kicked out ten head of yearlings we missed last year. They musta' held up along that creek bed they were carryin' pretty good flesh. Feed musta' been better in there most of the year."

Levi nodded his head "Yeah that country is really broken up in there. You're lucky to even spot 'em when they get in that brush. They get so cagey it's damn hard to get 'em outa' there."

"Y'know, one time Dad had a cowboy who tried to get some steers outta' that big arroyo and he never came out. Hell the next year we found a skeleton with a hat on it's head sittin' on the skeleton of a horse. It was hung up in a big Mesquite. That cowboy still had a loop built in his soga."

"Damn it Levi, don't be scarin' the boys like that. We never will get them to ride with us again."

" Zeb, that's the Gods truth so help me."

"Zeb's right Dad you'll have the boys wantin' to help the gals in the kitchen instead of cowboyin'."

Levi put a gut hook into the side of the bay gelding and headed off the grassy knoll towards the cattle. "Come on boys let's get this bunch down to the trap. We'll sort the calves off in the mornin'."

Randy looked over at Andy "Hopefully Dad will let me stay and give y'all a hand with the brandin'."

The cowboys continue to bunch the cattle and drive them towards the holding trap. Zeb rides out to the left to turn them back toward the Texas Gate. Jake stayed to the right of the herd to keep them from turning back as Zeb drove them toward the gate. Levi and the boys rode drag and kept the cattle moving at a slow but steady pace.

As they rode along Levi began to tell the boys about the ranch. "Ya know boys when my Great-Granddad put this ranch together he really knew what he was a doin'. He really wanted to leave something for his family."

Randy looked over at Levi with a puzzled expression on his face. "Granddad how is that he came to this part of Texas?"

6

"Well, it's like this: After the War for Southern Independence, his family's farm in Southern Georgia, got sold off to some Carpetbaggers cause they couldn't pay the taxes. All they had was Confederate shinplasters and that was only good for outhouse dabbin'. He had a pretty short fuse and he ended up shootin' two of 'em. It got pretty hot around there for him so he lit a shuck for Texas. When the dust cleared he was able to claim the hundred and sixty acres where our headquarters sits now."

Andy looked at him. "Yeah but we have more than a hundred and sixty acres on the ranch now don't we?"

"Yep. There's ninety-eight sections of good grazin' country now. A lot of his neighbors either starved out or were killed off by the Commanch. He stayed and fought 'em off the country he was aquiren' from folks who starved out or were killed. By the time the Lord called him home he left his family a damn well stocked spread with plenty a grass and water."

Randy shook his head in amazement. "He musta' been one tough hombre."

Levi nodded. Sure was. "He was as tough as a two bit steak. Durin' the war he rode with Captain Lesley, in B Company of the Confederate Special Cavalry. They were the fellas' that kept control of Confederate cattle herds."

"They got in many a fight runnin' off those Yankee rustlers. He got wounded three times, but they weren't able to kill 'im. Later they began to call his outfit the Cow Cav. You ever heard the expression Cracker? Most folks think it's some sorta name for folks from Georgia. In a way it is. Those boys in the Cow Cav used to drive cattle by cracking bull whips over their backs. The cracking sound would keep 'em moving. Folks started callin' them Crackers."

"Like I was tellin' you, when Bobby Lee surrendered at Appomattox Courthouse in 65, Granddad went home to Berrien County, only to find his family farm in ruins. Weren't nothin' left. The house was burned to the ground and the fields laid fallow. When the Carpetbaggers moved in and stole the place that's when all hell broke out. Later he got here to Texas and figured he'd go into the cattle business since that was all he'd done for the last two years."

"They say he was pretty shifty with a deck of cards and after he sold some cattle, he'd head to New Orleans' to try his luck at the tables. Supposed to have picked up some Yankee gold pieces on those river boats. Others say he and some of his old Cow Cav compatriots robbed a Yankee bank up in Ohio. Don't matter none now, hell it's all water under the bridge and he stocked the spread with plenty a good cattle."

Jake rode up to where Levi and the boys were talking as they drove the cattle. "What the hell is goin' on back here? We need to get this bunch to the trap before dark."

Levi looked over at him. "Just a little history lesson for the boys". Randy perked up "Yeah, Granddad was telling us how we came to be here."

Jake shook his head "We won't be here long if we don't tend to business and from the looks of things the good doctor is here, must have somethin' on his mind seein's how this is the first time in a year he's come out." Jake spun his horse around and rode back at a lope to turn the leaders into the holding trap.

Levi nudged the bay with a gut hook. "Come on boys lets tend to business before we get sacked." He and the boys continued to drive the cattle into the trap. The dust kicked up behind the herd as they began to trot through the Texas Gate. The men rode into the trap behind them as Jake stepped of his buckskin to close the barb wire gate. As the sun went down there was an orange glow through the dust.

Jake and Zeb rode through the cattle to settle them down a little and to watch them as the calves mothered up. "Looks like they handled the drive pretty well," Zeb said. "Yeah, Zeb sure does. These Corriente calves are pretty hearty." "Sure as hell are, I think they could live off a burnt tumbleweed."

As Jake and Zeb rode out of the trap the others unsaddled their horses at the tack room and carried them in. They turned their horses into a large corral and watched as the horses walked over to a large water tank. Jake and Zeb rode up dismounted and proceed to unsaddle their mounts.

Levi greeted them. "Hey Zeb, how about helping me throw out some hay to these horses. They've had a long day."

Jake said, "Dad you go on in with the boys, Zeb, and I'll take care of things out here. I'm not in a big hurry to see the good doctor anyhow."

The horses milled around in the dusty corral as Jake and Zeb began to throw out the Coastal Bermuda. A couple of the horses were rolling trying to dry the sweat from their backs. As they got up they shook their bodies and dust flew' from them.

Levi and the two boys walked slowly towards the house. It's been a long tiring day and they are ready for some grub and a shower. As they walked into the house they caught the aroma of freshly baked biscuits. A hint of chili beans and pot roast filled the air as well.

They walked into the front room and there stood Randy's Dad: Dr. Samuel Blevins, his face red with anger and his eyes glared through Randy like lasers. Disgusted he confronted Randy. "Why in the world didn't you drive back to town Sunday night? Your mother and I were very concerned about you not getting to school Monday. Here it is Thursday night and I've had to drive clear out here to find out what is going on. What gets into you son?"

"Dad, you know they're branding out here. They need all the hands they can get. I just thought I'd be of more use here than in school. Besides, Easter Break starts tomorrow and school will be out till the end of April. I've only missed four days this week. One more won't make a difference."

"Four days? Four days? Do you know what that could do to your scholarship potential? You could lose out if your grades don't hold up!"

Randy looked at the floor, cowed and humiliated from the tongue lashing.

Levi had heard all he could take. "Look Sam, why don't you cut the boy some slack? He was just tryin' to make a hand for us. Hell, you know how it is this time a year."

Samuel cut Levi off with disgust in his voice. "Yeah Dad, I know only too well how it is. I remember not getting to do a lot of things because of this Godforsaken ranch. Hell, we worked like dogs for you. For the life of me I don't know why Jake stays here. He's got a good education and could be an Ag teacher or extension agent. He doesn't have to work himself and Andy like this. God knows Kathy and Sally Ann would rather be living in town and not fifty-five miles from the nearest grocery store.

Jake walked into the house. "Well, howdy Doc! What's new down at your butcher shop? Been cuttin' off any arms or legs lately?"

"Damn you Jake, my work is for the betterment of medicine. What I'm doing is of no concern of yours. Besides, I'm here to get Randy back to town, not discuss concepts you can't even understand."

Jake shook his head. "Sam, why don't you give it a break? We don't really care what your doing for medicine! We're just tryin' to hold things together on this ranch. Cattle prices aren't the best and everything we buy is goin' up. I'm surprised people aren't goin' to town in wagons or on horseback gas is so high."

"I really don't have time to argue with all of you. Randy get your things together and get back to town."

"Aw, Dad, what's one more day of school anyway? Spring Break starts tomorrow, besides there's a lot of work to do here and school will be out till the end of April."

Levi, having once again had enough erupted. "Sam, you always were bull headed about a lot of things. Why don't you let the boy stay? It won't be the end of the world if he misses one more day. Besides they probably won't do much tomorrow anyhow. Kids just play grab-ass the last day before a vacation. You know how that is for sure! We need all the help we can get this year. Maybe you'd like to pitch in a little or would a couple of blisters ruin your golf swing?"

Randy again began to plead with Samuel. "Come on Dad...let me help with the brandin'. We'll be done by the time school starts again."

Dr. Blevins looked around the room at all of them staring at him like he was the Grinch that stole Christmas past. Knowing he was defeated he finally gave in. "All right, I guess it won't do much harm at this point. Hell, you've missed most of the week anyhow. I'll have to cover this with your mom and you know what that means. She can get her dander up pretty damn fast over things like this." He pointed his finger at Randy. "And you better not forget when school starts again and you *better* be in town in plenty of time to get yourself ready to hit the books again."

Without acknowledging anyone else, Dr. Blevins looked at Randy sternly then turned and walked out of the house to his car.

With a sigh of relief Levi looked at Kathy. "What do you and Sally Ann have to feed these tired hard-workin' cowboys? It sure smells good whatever it is." They all headed for the big dinning room table to enjoy the fine meal.

As they ate they began to hash over the next day's work load–another full day of working cattle.

Chapter 2

At 4:15 a.m.: Kathy and Sally Ann had been cooking since 3:30. The aroma of fried bacon, eggs, and fresh baked biscuits permeated the air, along with the smell of freshly brewed coffee. Just the stuff a crew of cowboys need to fuel their bodies for a long day of strenuous work.

The older cowboys were working on their second cup of hot C' when the two boys with tired, aching sore muscles staggered into the kitchen.

Jake scowled. "Hell boys, I thought you'd deserted us."

"Cut us some slack, Dad. We're not used to this."

Zeb set his porcelain cup down. "I remember when you were about these boys age, you had a rough mornin' now and then. Wasn't till you came back from the 'Nam that you made it to the table before Levi and me."

"Yeah, Charlie had a way a wakin' us up over there. Never could sleep much after that. Just hope these boys don't have to get those wake up calls."

They all began to fill their plates with the bountiful breakfast fixings. The muffled sound of chewing and few words is all that could be heard from the men at the table. They waste no time finishing their breakfast and began to leave the kitchen.

Levi grinned. "Ladies you done it again. Thanks for your fine cookin' it'll go a long ways today."

"No problem, Pop, we have to take care of our men."

The cowboys headed to the big corral to catch and saddle their horses.

"Boys I got it figured like this," Levi said. "We'll put all the cows and calves in the big corral and sort 'em in the alley. Zeb while we're sortn' you get the brandin'pot goin'."

Zeb headed to get the branding pot and heated the irons while Levi and the others sorted the calves off the cows.

Levi yelled "Boys, move around 'em!"

The leaders took the gate and soon the cows and calves were in the corral. They sorted some into the alley. Andy took the gate leading into the branding pen and Randy took the gate to the holding trap. Jake began to sort off the calves. Soon the branding pen was filled with the deafening sound of of bawling calves

"Man those calves sure don't want to be away from their mommas, do they?"

"That's just life, Randy. Nobody likes bein' separated from their mom. I saw many a tough soldier weep when he'd get a letter from his mom back in the world. These calves have some of the same feelin's I'm sure."

The irons were hot and syringes filled with the four way vaccine when Levi rode the bay into the branding pen. He built a loop double hocked a bull calf and headed to the flankers.

Jake headed to where the boys had removed the rope from the calve's back legs and secured him from head to tail. He yelled —"HOT IRON!"

A plume of white smoke rose off the left hip of the calf as the 7J/ seared into the hide. The stench of burning hair and searing flesh filled the air.

"Man that's a smell you won't ever forget. Every year it takes me a week to get it out of my nose."

"I know what you mean Randy."

Jake returned with his razor-sharp knife and a can of smear, then reached down between the calve's back legs and sliced the bottom off the scrotum. With the skill of a surgeon he shaved down the seminal vessel and soon the calve's blood-covered testicles were in his hand. Quickly he dobbed smear on the empty bleeding scrotum. "Where's the can for these mountain oysters?"

Zeb brought an empty gallon bucket along with the syringe filled with four way. "Here you go Jake put 'em in this. They'll sure make some good eatin' later." Zeb leaned down and gave the calf the injection. "Yeah, they sure will" Jake said. "It's always a tasty reward after all this hard work."

The boys released the calf and he staggered away a little on the sore side of life. "Levi and I always say they'll feel better when it quits hurtin'. He used to sing 'em that old song '*It Only Hurts for a Little While*', but he never could carry a tune in a bucket."

Levi dragged heifer to the flankers. "Boys that went pretty good. Keep this up we'll be done with this bunch by mid-afternoon."

Randy wiped his face with his shirt sleeve. "Keep this up I'll be done by late-mornin'."

"Me too this is tougher than fightin' forest fire."

"Reminds me of runnin' wind sprints during two-a-days in August only twice as bad. I love that old man but he's a pusher. They say Rome wasn't built in a day but it would a been if he was runnin' the job!"

The steady flow of calves continued and soon Kathy and Sally Ann arrived at the branding pen. "We're finished in the kitchen. We put on some pot roast and beans for lunch Maria brought by some fresh tortillas when she returned Sally's dress."

Randy looked up. "Wow Aunt Kathy, that sure sounds good!"

Levi paused as he dragged another calf to the boys. "Howdy ladies!"

Kathy looked at Levi as the calf is flanked and the rope released from the calves legs. "Where can we fill in Pop?"

"Bless your heart we can sure use the help. You can take over the shots, Zeb can handle the irons, and Jake can go ahead with the cuttin'. Sally honey, you keep the syringes filled for your momma and replace the needles when they're bad."

Levi rode back over to the calves bunched in the corner and heeled another one then headed to the flankers. "Here you go, boys."

Randy grabbed the calf by the tail and pulled it to the ground as Andy held it down and pulled a front leg back to secure the front end. Then Randy removed the rope from the calf's back legs. "Who spells us?"

"No one, on this outfit ya' work your way up to the irons and draggin'. As you say in town we're the new boys on the block. The only reason Grandpa cuts Sally Ann some slack is 'cause she's a girl and he watches out for women folk, especially if they ain't kin. You know how he and Zeb wander off to the Lonely Bull Saloon every now and then when things slow down around here. Sometimes they even go down to Piedras Negras to drink tequila and chase whores. They're both so long in the tooth it's a wonder they can catch one."

Randy looked up at Andy. "Do you think they'd take us along sometime?"

"Never...know...maybe if we do a good job they'll take us on a run for the border!"

With the thoughts of an adventure to the border with their Granddad and Zeb, the boys put even more effort into the backbreaking work, sweat pouring off them as the hot midday sun beat down on them.

Levi brought up another calf as the boys slowly moved to flank it. "This'll be the last one. We'll take a break for some grub. Kathy you and Sally go ahead and get things ready. We'll be right behind you."

The crew finished up with the last calf and headed over to the barn where the women had set up a table with the noon meal. There was no time for a sit down meal in the house with work to be done. The cowboys grabbed a tin plate and silverware and moved down the line.

"What do we have to drink, Aunt Kathy?"

"Your pick, Randy, there's sweet-tea,coffee or water. The tea is in that cooler."

"Thanks!"

The cowboys tried to find what shade they could and sat on the ground legs folded. The only sound from the tired crew was the rattle of metal forks on tin plates and muffled chewing.

The two young boys sat there speechless, thinking of a grand adventure to Piedras Negras or the Lonely Bull Saloon when the branding was done.

Suddenly their daydreams were shattered by the words of the task master. "Okay boys off your butts on your feet out'a the shade and int'a the heat. We got work to do and it won't get done till we get at it."

The boys gathered themselves up and headed towards the branding pen at a slower gate than they had seven hours earlier. Jake and Zeb moved to their jobs while Levi tightened the cinch on the bay. Kathy and Sally gathered the dirty tin plates and utensils and headed back to the house to wash things up.

Levi rode back into the branding pen and roped another calf. Soon the last calf was branded. Without a word spoken Jake walked over and opened the gate leading into the holding trap while Zeb and the boys moved around the calves and pushed them through.

Levi sat the bay near the gate and put a knot in a heavy string for every calf that passed into the trap. "Looks like we worked a hundred thirty-five head today. Went pretty well. Keep this up we'll have this brandin' done in no time at all."

Jake looked up at him. "What do you think Dad? let 'em mother up tonight an' then take 'em to the Big Draw in the mornin'?"

"Yeah... we can catch a cup of hot C' and watch 'em for awhile to make sure we don't have any bleeders. If we do we can cut 'em out and doctor 'em with some blood stopper."

The cowboys watched the calves as they mothered up, the freshly cut bull calves moving at a slower pace than their sisters.

Levi looked at Zeb. "Don't see any that look suspicious do you Zeb?"

"Nah, they look like they come through it pretty good. Usually you have a couple that want to bleed on you. It's been a pretty good day. Hope things run this smooth from here on out."

"Yeah, we can't afford to lose any with cattle prices the way they are. Jake how 'bout you and the boys pitchin' some hay out? They could use a little more feed tonight after the chousing they got."

"Okay Dad... Come on boys let's get unsaddled. and get to it."

They led their horses over to the barn and unsaddled them, then headed for the pickup to go over to the hay barn. Zeb and Levi picked up the branding equipment and then unsaddled their horses at the tack room.

"Those boys worked pretty hard today, Zeb."

"Yep, they sure did, maybe we should take 'em on a run to the Lonely Bull sometime."

Levi nodded and grinned. "Good idea, Zeb."

Chapter 3

The early morning sun silhouetted the cowboys driving the freshly branded calves from the trap and through the barbwire gate. Dust kicked up by the cattle had an orange glow as the sunrise penetrated it.

Levi said, "Once we get these over to water we'll scatter them a little and head for the Big Brushy"

"Sounds like a plan to me Dad" Jake kicked the Buckskin a little and turned the leaders towards the Purdy Draw tank.

The cowboys continued to drive the cattle at a slow but steady pace. The calves were moving along well and didn't seem to be lagging. Levi hollered back to Andy and Randy. "They're moving fine boys let's hold 'em at that speed."

As the sun was rose over the distant hills. The men had been moving cattle for at least an hour. In the distance the surface of the Purdy Draw tank sparkled as the sun began to shine over the shallow water.

Jake loped back to the boys who were trying to maintain the pace so as not to chouse the calves. "Once we get 'em to the tank we'll let 'em drink and make sure they don't head back to the ranch."

"Okay Dad we'll sorta ease 'em down there and back off a little."

Jake nodded. "Now your thinkin'. You're gon'na make a hand one of these days." A grin came over Andy's face as his Dad turned the big buckskin and ride back to the head of the herd.

"Holy cow Andy, that's the first time I've heard your Dad say somethin' like that"!

"Yeah it set me back a little too."

Some of the cattle were drinking muddy water from the dirt tank while others walked out into the tank churning the water. The crew backed away and watched as they drank and milled around the area foraging for sprigs of dry grass.

Levi rode up. "Boys we better head over to the Big Brushy got plenty to do over there."

"Jake you and Zeb cut over to that lower gate and try to pick up what you can in the lower Brushy, I'll take the boys to the upper Brushy and we'll gather up there and meet you over by Squaw Peak with what we find. We'll take Pedro and Pata with us too."

The teams split up and Levi whistled to the two cow dogs. Pedro and Pata follow behind him and the boys. As they rode towards the Big Brushy the boys were full of questions. It wasn't often they had time alone with their granddad. "You know, Granddad I've been wonderin,' how it is that Zeb came to be such a big part of the ranch? He's been here ever since I can remember."

"Yep he's been here since before your dad and Jake were born... Do you boys ever study about World War Two in school?"

"Sure we have in U.S. History." Randy shook his head. "It sure must'a been a pretty bad time for folks."

"It sure as hell wasn't no walk in the park that's for sure. I was workin' here for Dad when I got my letter from President Roosevelt. Hell I was just eighteen... a wet behind the ears kid. I'd never been farther from the ranch than San Marcos to buy groceries and barbwire. They sent me to San Antonio to the induction center there."

"What did your Dad say when he found out they drafted ya'?"

"He was pretty damned mad. Anyhow when I got to the induction center I met Zeb."

"Had he been drafted too?" Randy asked."

"Yeah, he sure had. He was a year older than me and green as a gourd, just like me. They sent us to Ft. Bliss over in El Paso then to Camp Hood over in Kileene. We called it Guadakileen."

Andy piped in. "What did you do there?"

"They trained us to be tankers then they shipped us over to Germany. Zeb and I fought together till Hitler shot his-self in the head."

The boys began to sense the strength of the friendship between Zeb and their Granddad. What could forge a stronger bond than fighting side by side with another man day in and day out not knowing if you'd ever get home to your way of life as a cowboy? They were truly country boys in the wrong country.

Jake and Zeb were about twenty yards apart moving along through some mesquite. "Hey Zeb that's where I spotted those yearlin's the other day.

They may have joined up with some cows on the other side of that ridge back."

The cowboys rode around to the left and toped out on the ridge. "There they are Jake, down in that draw. Looks like they've joined up with those cows you spotted." "Try to get around 'em Zeb and we'll bunch 'em up and push 'em toward where Dad and the boys should be."

Zeb made a wide circle so he wouldn't spook the cattle and the two men began to bunch them up. "Lookin' good Zeb let's try to head 'em over to the middle of the pasture."

Without saying a word the experienced old cowboy began to move them slowly in the direction they hoped to find Levi and the boys.

Levi and the two young cowboys were spread out and working their way through mesquite-filled arroyos gathering a couple of head at a time as they rode through the heavy thickets. Pedro and Pata were jumping cattle out of the heavier brush and bunching them up with the others. They had about thirty head moving through the arroyo when Jake and Zeb appeared over to their flank with seventy head or so. Soon the cattle were bunched up in one herd.

The cowboys were driving the cattle toward the gate when all hell broke loose. Wild hogs burst out of a mesquite thicket, running right through the middle of the cattle terrorizing them, and they scattered in five directions.

A big boar raced past Jake causing the buckskin to crow-hop. Jake grabbed the saddle horn. No time to be macho now. The rest of the cowboys spun their horses, trying to turned the cattle as they stampeded all around them. The terrified bovine looked like a covey of quail as they broke through the mesquite and topped out over the crest of the arroyo.

As things settled down Levi was visibly shaken. "Shit! Them damned no good for nothin' sons-a-bitches cost us a days work!"

"Sure as hell did Levi."

"If I had my Winchester I'd run 'em down and kill every damn one of 'em."

"Settle down you two. We'll round up what we can and come back and try again." Jake kicked the buckskin in the side and rode off to find as many of the spooked cattle as he could.

"He's right, let's gather what we can and get 'em down to the holdin' trap." Levi rode off and the others followed hoping to at least pick up the majority of the wild eyed bovines.

The crew worked for a couple of hours trying to recapture the cattle and ended up with fifty-five head. It was late afternoon when they started pushing them toward the Texas Gate. A couple of the cows tried several times to turn back.

"Looks like those two cows lost their calves in that ruckus."

"Yeah, let 'em go. Hell, we don't want to lose any calves; this has been enough of a wreck already. We'll get these down to the trap and come back Monday and try again. This damn pasture always is a bastard to gather.' Ever since I was a kid I dreaded workin' it."

The cowboys continued to drive the cattle and soon arrived at the gate. Jake rode ahead to open it and the cattle ran through into the trap. The cowboys rode toward the corrals to unsaddle for the day.

"Zeb, whaddya' say we make a run into the Lonely Bull tonight? I could use some cactus juice after this fiasco."

"Sounds good to me Levi. Soon's I get the mesquite thorns outta' my legs and take a hot shower I'll be ready to do some two steppin'."

"Y'think we should let these two boys tag along"?

"Hell, I think that's a splendid idea Levi. They need to experience somethin' 'sides playin around out here. Whaddya' say, boys? Feel like taggin' along with a couple old moss horns like us?"

The boys couldn't believe their ears. They were actually being asked if they wanted to tag along with their Granddad and Zeb.

"You're welcome to come along too Jake."

"No thanks Dad I think I'll stay around and keep an eye on these cattle. 'Sides I need to spend some time with Kathy."

After the day they'd had in the Big Brushy Jake couldn't believe the two old cowboys would have the energy to run the alleys in Austin.

"Well, boys are you up for some time in town?"

Randy piped up. "Are you kiddin', Grand-dad? sure we are!"

The cowboys rode into the corral and over to the tack room. Soon the horses were unsaddled and in the corral eating Coastal Bermuda.

The two young cowboys double-timed it to the house to hit the rain locker and put on a clean pair of Wranglers, shirt and their best pair of boots. They couldn't believe they were actually making a run with Grandpa Levi and Zeb, the two wildest cowboys they knew.

Chapter 4

Randy and Andy were waiting on the front porch as the two old cowboys walked out the front door. "Ready to head out?"

"Sure are, Granddad!"

"Well, let's get high behind."

They headed toward the dust-covered crew cab dualie. The pickup started down the dusty dirt road taking the two young cowboys on their first adventure with the two worldly cowboys.

"What y'think... should we stop off at Lu Lu's Bar-B-Q for a little grub? We might need somethin' in our bellies before we head to the Lonely Bull."

"Sounds good to us!"

"Levi I heard the Bunkhouse Boys are playin' there tonight."

"Who are they Zeb?"

"Sure ain't one of 'em rock bands, that's for damn sure boys."

Levi chimed in. "They're a bunch that travel from New Mexico to Nashville playin' some of the best country music you'll two step to. You know ,the old stuff like Earnest Tubb and Hank did...plenty of fiddle playn', an' one of 'em has some pretty good pipes and carries a tune."

Randy asked with doubt in his voice, "Do they play any hard rock?"

"Hell no! Zeb and me don't cotton to that crap!"

Zeb added "If you cain't two step to it we don't spend our dinero on it. 'Sides, we're Rye and tequila men."

Time passed fast with tales of the good old days keeping the boys spellbound. "Remember that time down in Juarez when we had that tequila shot game goin', Zeb? Old Allen was with us remember? Too bad he got killed by that bull in Tucson he was a hoot on the road."

"Yep, how could I forget that? We'd put a buck on the bar and each get a shot of tequila. You had to shoot it down without leavin' any in the bottom of the shot glass. The last man to do it kept the dinero on the bar. It took us awhile..."

Andy couldn't believe what he was hearing. How could someone sit there and down shots of tequila one after another? "Well, who won?"

Zeb slowly answered, with disgust in his voice. "Levi of course. We got ready to leave and he stepped off the bar stool an' fell smack dab on his face. Me an' Allen had to get 'im up to get 'im outta the place."

Levi shook his head. "I sorta remember that."

Zeb continued. "Yeah we were holdn' him up, one of us on each side of 'im. He had an arm around Allen's shoulder and one around mine. It was all we could do to keep him standn' good enough to stagger outta' the place.

We got 'im out on a sidewalk crowded with Mexicn's and started walkn' towards a cab. 'Bout that time an old taco vender came up and put a tray of tacos and tamales right in front of your old Granddad an' says,' 'Tacos hombres Tamales quede tacos?" Well, Levi looked down and let out a stream of used tequila all over him and his tray of tacos!"

The boys wide eyed and shocked at what they were hearing. They just couldn't picture their hero doing something like that.

Levi was gripping the steering wheel tightly ,hoping Zeb would end the story.

Seeing Levi's stress, Zeb wasn't about to let his old buddy off the hook. "Yep, that poor old Mexican just looked up at us totally mortified and said 'Too mush tequila eh?'"

Disgusted, Levi said "Hell. He probably sold 'em as tequila-flavored tacos."

Zeb continued. "We loaded Levi in the back seat of 1950 Chevy cab and he puked all the way to the line. That Mexican cab driver took the fastest route to the border that night! Then we loaded 'im in the back of the pickup so he wouldn't give us a tequila bath up front and headed to the motel down on Mesa. He felt that night for a couple a days."

The boys took it all in and were in a state of semi-shock as the pickup entered the Austin city limits and headed for Lu Lu's Bar-B-Que.

As Jake walked into the house, Kathy said, "Where you been honey?"

"Out at the barn. Thought I'd check things out and do a little thinkn'. You know I've been watchin' Randy a lot since he's been out here helpn' us. He's got a lot a natural ability when it comes to ranch work. It's like he's a clone of Dad. He looks just like Dad did in those old photographs. His mannerisms are just like him too. It's sorta scary watchin' the two of 'em sometimes."

"I know what you mean he's a lot like Levi for sure. Didn't your Dad have a chance to play professional football?"

"Yeah, but he got drafted into the Army and wasn't able to play. When he got home after the war thing's weren't going all that well so he helped his dad here on the ranch. He roped calves some and his winnin's helped out a little. He'd been a Turtle before he went overseas."

"Didn't the Turtles get professional rodeo started back in the thirties?"

"Yep they sure did, but they didn't make the money they do today. If they had we wouldn't be havin' the problems we are now. Y'know I sure wish Samuel would take more interest in the

34

ranch. I know Randy would be happy if he'd work with us. All he thinks about is his medical work."

The men in the dualie were pulling into the Lonely Bull Saloon parking lot.

"That sure was some fine bar-b-que grand-dad."

"Yeah, it'd make you want to slap your grandma!"

"Be careful now Levi."

As they pulled in the boys peered out the windows. The parking lot was jammed. A big neon sign of a bull with its head hanging down read *The Lonely Bull Saloon*.

Levi found a spot and parked the dualie and the boys quickly dismounted and paused, waiting for Levi and Zeb to catch up with them.

"Slow down boys. You don't want them buckle bunnies thinkn' your tryin' to snort in their flanks too soon."

Levi and Zeb grinned at each other as they watched the boys and enter the bar. The air was filled with the haze of colored neon lights filtering through cigarette smoke.

Levi grinned at the bouncer. "Howdy Frank. How's it goin'?"

"Where you two been? Haven't seen you in a while."

"We been pretty busy brandn'."

Frank looked at the boys. "I know you two old farts are legal, but who are these two?"

Levi said. "Watch who your callin' old farts. Frank, I'd like you to meet my two grandsons, Randy and Andy. They been workn' their butts off at the ranch so Zeb and me thought they needed a night of neon and perfume. What better place than the peaceful surroundin's of the Lonely Bull. There're more buckle bunnies here than any joint in this part a Texas."

"That's fine Levi, but how old are they?"

"Old 'nough to know the difference' t'ween a heifer and a cow, for sure."

"That's what I figured. You know the rules around here. They have to wear these wrist bands and cain't order nothin' stronger'n lemonade."

"No problem. They just want to shine their buckles. Won't have no problem with 'em."

The boys watched their fast talking Grand-dad, then followed him and Zeb to a table near the bar and dance floor.

"Looks like a good vantage point. Whaddya think Zeb?"

"Fine by me Levi."

As the four cowboys sat down, they began to read the room. A shapely blond waitress holding a tray walked up to the table. "What'll it be fellas?"

Levi nodded. "Well, I think me and Zeb here will start off slow, a couple shots of tequila and a Lone Star chaser. Lemonade for the boys will do."

As she stared sternly down at the two young cowboys, they looked up at a pair of nicely reconstructed mammaries struggling to stay within a tight fitting sequined top. "Hope you two old geezers don't have anything in your boots! You know these two can't be drinkin'!"

"Old geezers, Levi where does she get off callin' us old geezers?"

As she walks away the crew looked over the dance floor. The Bunkhouse Boys were playing *"Waltz Across Texas."*

Soon the shapely waitress returned with two shots of tequila, two Lone Star longnecks and a couple of lemonades. "That'll be eleven dollars."

Levi pulled a money clip out of his Wranglers and put fifteen dollars on the alcohol stained tray. "Keep it and keep 'em comin'."

She looked at the bills and turned to walk away. "Thanks, boys."

The two old cowboys held up their shot glasses brimmed with cactus nectar. "Here's mud in your eye."

"May your pony never stumble."

The boys watched as the old cowboys slugged down the tequila. Zeb looked around, then reached into his boot pulled out a small flask and quickly filled the two shot glasses, then slid it back into his boot, and looked at the boys. "We've been doin' this ever since we came home from the war. It's easier on the money clip."

As they watched the couples dance they nursed their longnecks and sipped at the bootleg tequila.

Zeb spotted a pretty young cowgirl sitting with friends. Without a word he walked over to her table. "Like to dance?"

She looked up at the grizzled old cowboy and smiled. "Why yes, thank you."

Zeb walked her out to the dance floor and began to two step. He was light on his feet and the young cowgirl was delighted. "You sure know how to dance cowboy."

"Had a lot of practice over the years."

"What's your name?" "Zeb. What's yours?"

"Ruth."

"Ruth, I'm pleased to meet you." They continued to dance as Levi walked over to the table. He asked one of the young gals to dance.

"Can you believe that Andy? We've only been here fifteen minutes and those two are already hooked up."

"Yeah. Looks like they've done this before."

"Those stories we heard about 'em chasin' Fraulines in Germany and Mexican whores in Piedras Negras must'a been true!"

Levi escorted his partner back to her table and then walked over to where the two stunned boys were sitting.

"Come on. They've asked us to join 'em." The boys followed Levi as he picked up the longnecks and headed toward where the young gals were sitting.

"Girls I'd like you to meet these two fine young cowboys. They're helpn' me and Zeb brand durin' their Easter break from school."

The boys pulled up some more chairs and sat their lemonade on the table. "They're in trainin' for some sorta sports, so they don't imbibe. We thought they needed some excitement so we brung 'em to town. This one's Randy and that knothead's Andy."

The girls gave the boys a once over and decided they were a little wet behind the ears for them, but were cordial as Ginny introduced herself. "I'm Ginny. This is Ruth and she's Mindy."

The boys acknowledged the introduction at the same time, "Pleased to meet you."

"Ginny, you girls come in here much?"

"Not really. We're grad-students at the University of Texas. We don't have much time to get out."

Mindy spoke up. "Unfortunately we spend a great deal of time on our studies. You know, 'Hook em Horns'."

Randy looked over at Ginny. "What ya'll studyin'?"

"I'm working on a PHD in Education Administration, Ruth's working on her MBA and Mindy is getting an MS in Range Management."

Zeb, in an undertone "We got some range she can manage..."

The boys sat there listening to Levi and Zeb spin their yarns about chasing wild cattle on the Llano River and going down the road roping and riding saddle broncs.

Randy tried to change the subject. "Boy that band is pretty good. They remind me of a band I heard on that station that plays old stuff."

Ruth quickly answered. "That song is 'Maidens Prayer.' It's one of my favorites, would you like to dance Randy?"

"Why sure!"

As they walked out onto the dance floor, Zeb watched them with disgust. "'Maidens Prayer' all right. I dance with her an' then she asks him to dance. 'Maidens Prayer' my skinny ass. He's pullin' the same crap on me that you used to, Levi."

Levi excused himself and headed for the outhouse as Andy continued to make small talk with Ginny. "That's a good band, for sure. I hear they're from New Mexico."

"Yes, they are. We try to make it out here when they have a gig here."

"Have they been playin' together long?"

"I've heard they started playing together when they were in high school. They worked on their Uncle Dell's ranch and took up playing songs they listened to on the *Louisiana Hay Ride*. I guess they lived in the ranch bunkhouse so people started calling them the Bunkhouse Boys."

"They sure know what they're doin'."

As the night wore on the conversation continued and the girls continued to trade dances with the four cowboys. At close to one a.m. the bartender yelled, "LAST CALL FOR ALCOHOL!"

Ginny looked up at the clock on the wall next to the bar. "Well, I guess we'd better get going, girls. It sure was nice meeting y'all."

The others concurred. "Hopefully we'll see y'all here again sometime."

Levi stood up as they collected their belongings. "Why yes that would nice."

Zeb sat there disgusted. "Yeah, bet you would. We done spent fifty dollars on drinks for you and didn't even get kissed."

The four dejected cowboys finished off their longnecks and lemonade. As they got up to walk out Levi staggered a little.

Frank the bouncer was standing near the door watching the crowd as they walk out. "Levi maybe you better let one of them lemonade drinkers drive. Looks like old Jose Cuervo has the best of you."

"Mebbe yer' right pard'. I could-use a siesta."

Levi reached in his pocket pulled out the keys and pitched them to Randy.

As they walked out the door Levi and Zeb were moving a little slower than the boys and had a stagger in their step. The two old cowboys piled in the back seat of the dualie and conked out as Randy drove toward the Austin city limits and the ranch. "Man, Randy, this wasn't as big a deal as I thought it would be. I sorta thought we'd find some girls more our age. Those college gals were sure lookers but I don't think we fit their bill."

"Yeah but it'll get better when they take us to Piedras Negeras. That has to be a wild place for sure. Those muchachas' are real lookers. Granddad says they make you want to throw rocks at the gals over here."

The dualie moved down the highway and then cut off on the dusty dirt road back to the ranch. The sun would break over the rolling hills shortly, and it would be another rough day gathering the Big Brushy.

Chapter 5

Morning came to soon. Flashbacks of the night at the Lonely Bull danced in the boy's minds as they finished their biscuits and sausage gravy. Suddenly a jolt of reality hit them. A day of hard riding in the Big Brushy was waiting. It hadn't gone well the last time they went in there. Gathering the Big Brushy was unpredictable at best. Now they are tackling it again on three hours of sleep.

Kathy and Sally Ann were putting together some machaca burritos for the cowboys to carry in their saddlebags. They'd need some nourishment to help them make it through the long day. The boys got up and were headed out of the kitchen when Kathy stopped them. "Boys here's some lunch for you. Give some to the others."

"Okay, Mom. No problem."

The boys picked up the flower sacks containing the machaca burritos and headed to the barn. "Good to see you two could make it. Catch up your horses and get saddled. We're burnin' daylight."

Andy tilted his head to the sky. "There ain't no daylight to burn Granddad."

"Well, let's make sure we don't burn any when it gets here. We need to be in the Brushy by first light or we won't get it gathered today."

Levi stepped into the stirrup and swung his right leg over the cantle and sat up straight as he hit the saddle. "Well come on. Let's get the led out!"

Randy looked around in the dark. "Grandpa, where's Jake and Zeb?"

"They lit out fifteen minutes ago. They didn't want to wait on you two. 'Sides they had to check the cattle in the holdin' trap."

Levi and the boys hit a long trot as they rode to meet up with the others. Jake spotted them as they rode up. "Howdy boys. Where you been?"

"How do they look, Jake?"

"They're doin' pretty damn good seein's how bad they got choused."

The crew rode through the cattle on their way to the Texas Gate that secured the entrance to the Big Brushy. "Dad it looks like you're still feelin' that cactus juice. You boys must'a had quite a time."

Levi cleared his throat. "Yeah, it got intense. Randy there really cut a rug with that little college gal."

Randy grinned. "I thought you two would be feelin' better by now. That tequila must'a been pretty powerful!"

Levi scowled. "Back off Randy, I got on my horse all right."

Zeb cleared his throat and spit out a green wad. "Yeah, Levi I just hope you can stay on 'im.

.Ya' ain't the stud you used to be. That stuff hits you harder at your age."

The crew gets to the Texas Gate just as the sun started to break over the distant hills.

Randy trotted up to the barbed-wire gate, jumped off his horse and opened it, allowing the others to ride through. They rode up a little then waited for him to close the gate and catch up.

Jake looked at Levi. "Dad, how do you want us to work it today?"

"Got it figured like this, you head over to the backside of the pasture on the Southeast. The rest of us will fan out to the north of you. We'll pick up cattle as we move back this way and bunch 'em here at the gate and drive 'em on over to the holdn' trap. Hopefully we'll get most of 'em in one pass. We can come back for any we miss tomorrow."

Jake headed southeast and the others fanned out and headed to the back side of the Brushy. The country was rough with deep, mesquite filled arroyos. They moved through the terrain slowly, knowing a bad step could cause a wreck in a split second.

As they rode they spotted some of the cattle they'd spilled when wild hogs had spooked them the day before.

Pedro and Pata followed behind Levi as he slowly worked his way along the crest of a steep, mesquite filled arroyo looking for cattle. He didn't see the undercut bank. The bay sloughed off the bank and lost its' footing then fell, pinning Levi under him as he slid and tumbled down the steep wall into the arroyo He finally crashed to a bone-jolting stop in a heap, pinning Levi to the floor of the arroyo. The bay slowly got to its feet, dizzy, skinned, and cut; but with nothing broken. He stood there looking down at Levi lying there dazed and moaning.

Levi's chaps were torn from his legs, and one leg was twisted at a forty-five degree angle behind his back with a jagged end of the femur protruding from his torn, blood-soaked pant leg. His left arm was bent from his shoulder to the wrist in an unnatural position. He drifted in and out of consciousness, unable to move. The two faithful cow dogs lay next to him their heads resting on the ground.

The rest of the crew had made it to the backside of the Brushy and were combing their way back picking up cattle as they moved through the mesquite toward the Texas Gate. As the mid-afternoon sun passed over the tired sweaty cowboys began to arrive at the Texas gate at intervals bunching the cattle. The cattle began to mill around as the boys held them together.

Jake grinned. "Looks like we have a little over a hundred Zeb."

"Yeah... wonder what Levi picked up?"

"Don't know, have you seen 'im'?"

"Not in awhile. Last time I seen him he was headed toward the back side 'bout a hundred-fifty or so yards to the north of me."

"That's up near that big arroyo isn't it?"

Zeb nodded. "It sure as hell is Jake.

Maybe we should ride back up there and see if we can find 'im." Jake turned to the boys. "Andy, you two stay here and hold these together. Zeb and me'll ride back and see what's holdn' Dad up."

The boys stayed back a little from the cattle and rode slowly back and forth around them keeping them bunched up close to the fence.

At a long trot, Jake and Zeb headed toward the big arroyo where Zeb had last seen Levi. As they approached the arroyo they heard barking and shrill whining coming from the two cow dogs. Slowly they worked along the bank of the arroyo looking for signs of Levi and the howling dogs.

"Damn, Zeb, there he is!"

"Sure as hell! Let's get down there pronto!"

It's rough going down the steep arroyo walls as they inched their way through the thick mesquite, trying to get to Levi as quickly as they could. At last they were able to move along the arroyo floor and arrive at Levi, who was laying there unconscious.

Jake quickly dismounted and stumbled toward Levi. He knelt beside him.

"Dad? Dad can you hear me? Can you hear me Dad?"

Levi moaned.

Zeb leaned over. "Thank God he ain't dead, but he's in damn bad shape! Levi... Levi, you son of a bitch! Don't you die on me, you hear?"

Jake looked around frantically. "What the hell are we gonna do Zeb? How we gonna' get him out of this damn arroyo without killin' him? He's broke all t' hell!"

"Listen Jake don't you panic on me! This ain't the first storm Levi and me been in. We just got to use our heads! One damn thing for sure–we cain't put 'im on that horse. It'd kill 'im for sure. We'll have to do the next best thing."

"What do you have in mind Zeb?"

"Back in the old days the Indians used to move their wounded on a travoi. We'll make one."

They moved quickly, cutting limbs from mesquites with their knives. Jake took the lariats from their saddles, cut off the hondos and un-wound them.

"We can use these to tie the travois to-gether."

"Good thinking Jake!"

Zeb walked over to the bay, unsaddled him, tossed the saddle blankets over next to the sap-lings, and then re-saddled him, pulling the cinch up tight.

They quickly laid out the frame of the tra-vois and began lacing it together with strands of lariat. Zeb cut the tie strings from Levi's saddle and began to lace the saddle blankets to the mesquite limbs, which had been securely tied between two long, thick limbs. "Let's cut what's left of those chaps off him. We'll cut strips from 'em to help hold him in place."

"For sure we don't want him slidin' off the damn thing!"

The crudely constructed travoi was finally completed. The two men quickly ran the long limbs through the stirrups and tied them in place with what was left of their ropes.

"That'll have to do. Move it as close to Levi as you can."

Jake slowly led the bay toward Levi stopping the travois next to him. The uneven ground caused the men to struggle as they placed Levi on the saddle blankets. From deep within his unconscious state Levi let out a horrifying scream.

"Hell, Zeb, he's really hurtin'!"

"He damn sure is Jake. We're gonna have to take it slow gettn' outta here."

They secured Levi to the travois with some of the leather strips that they'd cut from his torn chaps.

"Well, Zeb it's time to cut bate. I'll lead him outta here. You ride ahead and tell Andy to get to the ranch pronto and tell Kathy to get a mattress in the back of the pickup. Run them cows into the holdin' trap and wait for me. Here take my horse with you."

He handed Zeb his reins and then began to slowly lead the bay forward trying to find his way out the best he could. He inched his way along the arroyo floor until he spotted a gentle incline that would allow the bay to pull the injured cowboy to the crest. Leading the bay, he moved cautiously forward, then headed toward the Texas gate. The ground was uneven, with rocks and shallow cuts, the slow-moving travois constantly jarring its injured cargo.

Levi drifted from an unconscious to semi-conscious state emitting moans of pain.

Zeb rode as fast as he could, leading Jakes horse toward the gate. As soon as he spotted the boys holding the cattle he yelled out, "Open the gate and run 'em through!"

Sensing something was wrong Andy circled the cattle and opened the wire gate as Randy started driving them through.

Zeb rode up dropped the reins to Jake's horse and helped push the last ones out of the Big Brushy.

"What's goin' on Zeb? Where's Dad and Granddad?"

"Levi had a hell of a wreck over in that deep arroyo. He's busted up pretty bad. Jake and I had to make a travois to get 'im outta there. Your dad's bringn' him in."

"Andy, ride to the house and tell your mom that Levi had a bad wreck... to throw a mattress in the back of the truck to put him on so we can get him to town. We'll wait here for your dad and help him get Levi in."

Andy spun his horse and jabbed him in the belly with a gut wrench. The horse bolted forward and Andy sat him like a pony express rider being chased by wild Indians.

"Is Granddad goin' to be all right Zeb?"

Zeb shook his head. "Don't know. He's in bad shape. That old geezer better not die on me."

Jake led the bay pulling the injured cowboy to the gate and stopped. He was exhausted and fear filled his eyes. "Got any water in your canteen?"

"I do Uncle Jake!" Randy rode over to him and handed down the canteen.

Zeb looked at Jake. "Hell, I thought you'd never get here. How's he doin'?"

"Not all that well. He keeps moanin' with pain." Jake paused. "That's a damn long hike."

"It sure as hell is. The ride over here seemed to take forever too."

Randy rode over to get a better look at his Granddad. "My God what happened!"

"No time to talk about it now we gotta get him to the hospital."

"Andy rode ahead to tell Kathy to get ready. He lit outta here like a scared jackrabbit." Zeb said.

Jake looked back at the travois. "That's good … Sure hope she's ready when we get there."

He rested a minute and took another swig from the burlap-covered canteen. "Well, let's get goin'. We still have a couple miles to go."

"Want me to lead that horse awhile?"

"Nah, I'm Okay."

Slowly they began the trek to the ranch, hoping Levi would make it there alive, much less to the hospital some fifty-five miles away.

Chapter 6

Andy rode hard, his little sorrel horse was lathered and breathing hard as he rode into the ranch. Quickly he dismounted, and dropped his reins and sprinted toward the house.

"Mom... Mom!"

"What's wrong Andy!"

"Mom, Granddad's been hurt real bad!"

"What happened?"

"His horse fell into that big arroyo with him. He's hurt bad!"

"Where's your dad?"

"He's bringin' him in! I didn't see him. Zeb rode up to where Randy and I were holding the cattle we'd gathered and said for me to get here fast and tell you to get the pickup ready to take him to town! He said to put a mattress and blankets in the bed of the pickup."

Kathy moved quickly, stripping blankets from the bed in Levi's room as Sally walked in. "What's wrong Mom?"

"Help me with this Sally!"

Sally began helping her mother without any further discussion. They struggled to get the mattress out of the house and carried it to the pickup. Andy was cleaning out the bed of the pickup, and as quickly as he finished they threw the mattress in. "I'll get some blankets and we'll take the pickup down to the barn."

They waited anxiously, looking to the East for any sign that Jake and the others might be approaching.

"Do you see anything?"

"No, Mom, not yet."

"My Lord I hope they're all okay!"

"Don't fret Mom. They should be here soon."

Sally Ann didn't say a word trying to maintain control of her emotions. "Mom is Granddad going to be okay?"

"Honey, we just have to pray he is! I'm sure your Dad and Zeb are doing all they can to make sure he's okay."

In the distance they saw two men on horseback and another leading a horse that was leaving a faint dust cloud trailing behind it. "Look Andy, there they are! Thank God!"

As they drew nearer, Andy ran out to them.

"Let me take Dad's horse for you Zeb."

"Thanks, Andy."

As they entered the corral next to the barn, Jake continued to lead the bay over to the pickup.

"My God, Jake! What happened?"

"I don't have time to explain it right now. I'll tell you what I can about it later. Right now we need to get him to the hospital!"

Levi lay there motionless on the makeshift travois as they prepared to lift him onto the mattress.

54

"Okay we all have to lift together." As they lifted Levi onto the mattress he let out with a subconscious scream.

"Careful now. We can't afford to drop him."

The hundred eighty-five pound cowboy felt like a ton as they struggled to get him into the back of the pickup. Gently they placed him on the mattress and covered him.

"Did you call the hospital?"

"I had Sally call them while I was getting the pickup ready."

"That's good I hope they let Samuel know we're comin' in."

"She told them to. I'm sure they did."

"Zeb, you and Sally ride up front with me,"Jake said.

"Kathy and the boys can take care of Dad."

As the pickup sped down the bumpy dirt road Levi drifted from an unconscious to semi-conscious state, speaking deliriously. "Rita...Rita... are you there, Rita?"

"Whose Rita Aunt Kathy?"

"Boys, I don't think this is the time to go into that... I'll explain it to you later."

"There's a headstone up at the family cemetery that has Rita on it. Is that who he means?"

Kathy remained silent, as though she hadn't heard them.

Again Levi called out for Rita. In a soft voice Kathy replied "Yes, Levi... I'm here... just lay still."

In the distance they could see the lights of town. Jake looked at Zeb. "This is the longest trip in here I've ever made!"

"You're doin' fine cowboy just hang and rattle!"

"Damn, Zeb, I can't believe this has happened! Dad is always the most careful of us all!"

"Take it easy Jake. We need to get there in one piece!"

Dr. Samuel Blevins was standing in the emergency entrance watching for them as the dualie came to a screeching stop.

"Orderly, bring that gurney and follow me!"

As the orderly pushed the gurney toward the dualie a nurse quickly followed behind him. Jake was just getting out of the pickup.

"What the hell happened, Jake?"

"We were gatherin' the Big Brushy and Dad's horse took a fall."

The emergency staff quickly placed Levi on the gurney and started for the door.

"Get him to ICU, stat! Jake, I'll get back to you as soon as I can!"

They watched as Samuel followed the gurney down the hallway.

"Kathy, I'll go over and get Dad admitted. You take everyone to the waitin' room."

Jake headed toward Admittance as the little group, dazed with disbelief walked into the emergency waiting room and sat quietly staring at each other.

Randy said. "Aunt Kathy, I've been thinking about Granddad callin' out for Rita, Who is she?"

"Yeah Mom, who is she?"

With tightness in her throat not wanting to divulge Rita's identity, she hesitated. "Rita was your grandmother. Your Granddad never speaks of her. He carries a great deal of guilt about her passing. He truly loved her."

"How come he felt guilty about her? Was something wrong with her?"

"Believe me there was nothing but good in that lady! She was the real thing, the perfect rancher's wife. But Levi felt like keeping her at the ranch was what caused her death. Randy, after your dad was born Jake came along two years later. She had a difficult time delivering him and her doctor told her she shouldn't have anymore children."

"But she didn't. They only had Dad and Jake."

"Not exactly. Rita became pregnant again and she had a terrible time with the pregnancy. Levi wanted her to stay in town close to the hospital, but she insisted on staying at the ranch."

"She was probably afraid to let grandpa outta her sight." Andy said.

"No, that wasn't it at all. She just felt her place was taking care of the household. She was in her fifth month when she became very ill. Levi and the boys were staying at the line camp for a couple of days while checking cows. By the time they got back to the ranch she was in serious condition. They tried to get her into the hospital, but she died before they could get her to town."

"Wow! Dad never said a word about this to me."

"Your Grandpa went into a deep state of depression blaming himself for her death. It took him a long time to get back to normal. If it weren't for Zeb taking control of the situation, it would have been much worse."

Zeb was sitting close by, listening to Kathy tell the kids about Rita and Levi. "Y'know kids," he said.

"Things like that can make a man go plumb loco. I'm gonna tell you somethin' you already know; your Granddad is a strong man. When he finally put that all in its' place he put his heart and soul into raisin' his boys. Jake took to the ranch like it was his only chore in life. On the other hand Samuel blamed the place for the loss of his mother. He didn't want much to do with it."

Kathy interrupted for a moment. "When Samuel finished high school, Levi sent him to Johns Hopkins to study medicine, and Jake went to New Mexico State and studied Livestock Science and Range Management."

"Now I understand why Dad doesn't want to be a part of the ranch and why he doesn't want me to work out there either."

"I'm afraid that's true Randy. it's a shame he has those feelings about the place. I know Rita would have wanted him to be involved with it, especially now."

"I'll bet Grandma Rita was a fine lady!"

The little group sat there quietly, the youngsters trying to digest the newly discovered information about their Grandmother Rita.

Jake broke the silence. "Well, he's admitted, its' a good thing we all filled out those legal papers last year. With that power of attorney, I didn't have any problems."

Zeb said,"Yeah Jake, but I sure hate that you had to use it. Do you know how he's doing?"

Jake looked around the room at the others. "I'm not really sure. I know Sam is in there with the ER Doctor. I'm sure they'll tell us as soon as they know somethin'."

Zeb stood up and walked over to where Jake and Kathy were standing. "He's a tough one, and I know the Good Lord cares about him or he'd a been dead years ago. We just got to stick together on this. He'll sure need our support to pull this one off; that's for damn sure!"

Samuel and the ER doctor walked into the waiting room.

"I'd like all of you to meet Dr. Randall."

"Good evening, folks. I'm pleased to meet you. I know you want answers, so I'll be candid.

We've taken X-rays and done a CAT Scan. We are scheduling him for an MRI and other tests tomorrow... I don't want to minimize Levi's condition; he's experienced a great deal of trauma. You're going to have to be patient. It's going to be awhile before we have all of the test results."

Samuel spoke up. "The best thing we can do right now is let Dr. Randall and his team continue with their examinations. Dad is in good hands. All of you need to get back to the ranch. You need to rest and I know you have a lot more branding to do."

Zeb said. "Yeah, you're right Sam... not much we can do here."

"Dr. Randall and I will be working together on this, and rest assured I'll call you as soon as I have more information."

"Is there anything we need to bring in for him?"

"No, Mrs. Blevins, not at this time. We'll see to his needs. You just take care of your crew."

Dr. Randall said, "All of you did a fine job of getting Levi to us. We'll do all we can to make sure he gets the best of care."

Samuel shook Jake's hand. "Don't worry Jake, I'll watch over Dad. You just take care of things at the ranch. He turned to. Randy "You go on back with them. They're going to need all the help they can get. I'll square things up with your mom."

"Thanks, Sam," Jake said. "We really need his help. He's almost as good a hand as Dad...but don't tell Dad I said that, or he'll have my hide."

The tired little group headed out to the dualie for the long trip back to the ranch. There was plenty of work to be done and they're short handed.

Chapter 7

Morning seemed to come fast after the nerve-wracking day before and the long ride back to the ranch. At 6:30 Jake and Zeb were having an early morning cup of hot C. Kathy and Sally were rustling up a cowboy breakfast.

"Jake, I know you got a heap on your mind right now but we need to figure out how we're gonna' get the brandin' done."

Jake took a swallow from his mug. "I know Zeb. This has really set us back. We're gonna' need more help to get that Godforsaken' pasture gathered and the brandin' done."

"Maybe we should drive over to the Rafter V and talk to Old Man Knight. He might give us a hand."

"That's a good idea, Zeb. After we finish up here we'll drive over there. The boys can throw out some feed to those we managed to get in the holdin' trap yesterday."

As they finished up another fine breakfast the boys walked in looking tired and bedraggled, yawning and rubbing their tired eyes.

"Mornin' boys. Have a seat. Zeb and I've been discusin' the predicament we're in. We've decided to go over and see if we can get some day hands from Old Man Knight. We'll need for you to throw some feed out to the cattle in the holdin' trap and keep things organized around here today."

The boys sat down. Andy said,. "Sure, Dad, we can handle things around here okay. Has there been any word from Uncle Samuel?"

"No maybe he'll call later. Your Mom will let you know if there's any news."

"I'm sure Dad will call us as soon as he gets more information. He knows how worried we are."

Kathy walked over and filled the empty mugs. "I'm sure he will, we just have to be patient and pray that everything is going well. Samuel won't spare anything when it comes to Levi."

Jake finished his coffee and walked over and gave Kathy a peck on the cheek. "Thanks Honey. That was really a good breakfast."

He and Zeb walked out and headed toward the pickup, drove over and filled the tank, and then started the nearly falf-day trip to the Rafter V.

"You know, this accident couldn't have come at a worse time. The market isn't doin' all that great, and now Dad is busted up and there's no tellin' how he'll come out of it."

"Yep, an' it's gonna' get worse if we don't get some rain. Knowin' Levi like I do he'll be blamin' himself for everything that's goin' against us."

"Yeah, I know he will, 'specially if that health and accident insurance doesn't pay off. They're quick to take your money, but slow to pay off. I know Dr. Randall and Sam will do all they can to help, but the hospital bills will be considerable."

As they drove into the Rafter V headquarters they saw Old Man Knight down at the barn and drove over to where he was watching Javier and Carlos working with a three year old colt.

Jake said, "Well, here goes..."

They got out of the dualie.

"Howdy, Mr. Knight. Hola Javier y Carlos."

"What brings you boys way the hell over here?"

"Well Sir, we've come to talk to you 'bout a situation we're in."

"Where's Levi?"

"That's part of why we're here. We were gathern' the Big Brushy yesterday and Dad's horse took a bad fall with him."

"Is he all right?"

"Not exactly. He's in the hospital. Sam and a Dr. Randall are takin' care of 'im."

"Good God almighty! What are they sayin' 'bout 'im'?"

"They did some X-rays and a CAT Scan on 'im but..."

"What Jakes tryin' to say is that they don't really know what all is wrong with 'im yet. He has a broken leg for sure, but drifts in and out like he's got a head injury or somethin'."

"That's a hell of a note, boys. Is there anything I can do to help?"

"Well, yes there is, Mr. Knight. We need to finish gathern' and brandin' and we're short handed. We were wonderin' if we could get a little help?"

"Good Lord yes. Javier, Carlos and I'll be at your place at first light."

"Mr. Knight, I can't thank you enough. I know Dad will appreciate it."

"Let me tell you somethin' Jake. I'll never forget the consideration Levi and Zeb here gave me when my boy William was killed in Viet Nam. He seemed to know what I was goin' through, and he and Zeb were fine neighbors through it all."

Jake looked at Mr. Knight. "Well, thank you Sir. I appreciate you throwin' in with us."

"Thanks, Mr. Knight!"

"No problem Zeb. We'll see you in the mornin'."

Jake and Zeb shook Old Man Knight's hand and turned and walked back to the pickup not saying a word, knowing they would have three good hands to help them finish gathering the Big Brushy.

All they could hear as they drove along was the hum of the diesel engine.

"Y'know, I don't remember when William Knight was killed," Jake said. "I don't even remember goin' to his funeral."

"That's 'cause you weren't here. You were over in Nam."

66

"That seems like a lifetime ago, but yet there's times it's like it was just last week."

"I know what you mean. When Levi and I came back from Europe after World War Two it took us a long time to forget what happened over there. We were lucky to get home alive. Those Panzers' were knockin' off our Shermans' like they was nothin'!"

"Guess we were all pretty damn lucky, Zeb. It sure was good of Mr. Knight to remember how you and Dad supported him when his boy was killed."

"Yeah, I'd forgot all 'bout it: 'till he mentioned it."

Jake comments. "His family has been here since after the War of Northern Aggression also. They've become very successful."

"Yeah, they sure have. Old Man Knight has enough money to burn a herd of wet cows. 'But you wouldn't know it by the way he works. You'd think he was just one of the cowboys."

"That's for sure Zeb. There's no frills or fancy stuff with that man... just leather and grit."

As they drove into the ranch the sun was beginning to set in the West. Andy and Randy ran out of the house to greet them.

"How'd it go Dad?"

"Pretty good Son. Mr. Knight and his two cowboys Javier and Carlos will be here at first light."

"That's great. We'll have a great crew."

"That Javier is one of the best men I've ever seen with a young horse."

Zeb said. "You're right about that Randy. They don't get any better."

As night closed in they all sat on the front porch talking about the day and what lay ahead.

With a worried tone Jake committed. "I wonder why Sam hasn't called to let us know how Dads' doin'?"

Kathy squeezed his hand. "Honey, you know how Sam is, he'll want to be able to give us all the information he can when he calls."

"You're right. He won't call 'till he has all the test results. That'll probably take awhile."

"You cowboys better get some rest. You're going to have a long day tomorrow."

"That's for sure, Honey. It seems like the days just get longer and the work's un-endin'."

The tired little group said their goodnights and headed off to sack out for the night. Another hard day of gathering the Big Brushy lay ahead. Daylight would be there sooner than later.

Chapter 8

"Randy throw a loop on that little paint."

"Sure, uncle Jake. I've really been wanting to ride that one."

"Well, there's no time like the present to get 'er done."

Randy built a loop and walked into the large corral that held the remuda. He swung the rope, then tossed it over the paints head as though he was throwing a baseball.

Zeb grinned. "That was a hell of a loop Randy! You looked like Levi handlin' that soga like you did."

"Thanks, Zeb. He showed me how to throw a hoolihan, but it took a long time to get where I could."

He coiled the rope as he walked up to the paint, patted him on the neck and led him over to the tack room where the rest of the crew was saddling up.

Andy said, "Granddad tried to teach me that, but I couldn't get it down."

"You just got a keep practicn'."

Andy nodded. "Guess I better."

As they finished saddling their horses the vaqueros from the Rafter V pulled up to the barn. Javier and Carlos unloaded three horses that were saddled and ready to go.

Old Man Knight walked up to the Blevins' crew and held out his right hand.

"Mornin' boys." He shook Jake's hand.

"Mornin', Mr. Knight good to see you."

Javier and Carlos led the horses up to the barn. "Buenos dias,."

Zeb responded. "Buenos dias hombres."

Jake began to lay out the day as they listened intently. "Got it figured like this: we'll split up in teams, spread out and ride to the backside. That way we'll be able to keep an eye on each other in case there's a problem. That's tough country and we sure as hell don't want to get anyone else hurt. If someone gets in a storm we can get to 'em pronto."

"Good thinkin'. After what we experienced with Levi, we'd better keep an eye on each other."

Jake said, "Mr. Knight, I was thinkin' you and I would team up on the north end. Zeb and Carlos can work through the center and Javier could take the boys to the south corner of the pasture and work back."

"Sounds good to me; let's get at it."

The cowboys mounted up and headed toward the Texas Gate.

"'Bout how many do you think you have in here Jake?"

"I figure there may be close to a hundred ninety head of cows and calves, mostly Corrientes'. There's some commercial Hereford cows too. Dad crossed 'em on those Corriente bulls. He was wantin' to see how the calves handled this type of country."

"Levi's pretty smart runnin' those Corrientes'. They seem to hold their price when the rest of the markets down."

"He figures they're always gonna' want to do some doggin' and team ropin'."

"Levi sure as hell was a ropin' fool back in the old days."

"Yeah he sure was. He's really slowed down over the past couple years and now he's had this wreck no tellin' what's gonna' happen."

"If I know Levi and I believe I do, he'll come out a fightn'. He's a tough one and not one to quit."

"Sure hope your right, Mr. Knight...I sure do hope you're right!"

The teams split up as they rode through the Texas Gate.

"See y'all back here later. Good luck and be damn careful."

Zeb turned back in his saddle before he rode off. "Ya' know we'll be extra careful this go 'round."

The two young cowboys rode along with Javier and soon passed the big arroyo where Levi had taken his fall.

"Javier, that's where Granddad got hurt."

"Es muy malo, cuidado hombres."

"Si, Javier."

Soon the teams were on the backside of the Big Brushy and heading back toward the gate, picking up cattle as they moved through the mesquite. Pedro and Pata moved through the thick brush running the horned cows and their calves out so the cowboys could bunch them and head them toward the big Texas Gate.

By late afternoon the teams began to arrive at the Texas Gate. Jake and Mr. Knight were there with about sixty-eight head of cows and calves. The others began to show up with cows calves and a few yearlings.

"Lookin' pretty good, boys. We may have combed it pretty well this time."

Zeb rode over to Jake. "We picked up about ten head we missed last year."

"That's damn good." Jake looked over the yearlings. "Looks like they put on some size. They're showin' a little puerno."

Javier rode over got off his horse and opened the gate. Jake and Mr. Knight rode through and stopped off to the side of the open gate.

"Mr. Knight, would you count the calves? I'll get the cows and yearlins'."

The rest of the crew slowly moved the cattle through the gate so they wouldn't spill any. Old Man Knight and Jake sat their horses, taking a count as the cattle moved through the gate and began to mill around as they settled out.

The cowboys followed the last ones through. Randy jumped off the paint and closed the gate as the others circled the herd and started them toward the branding trap. Within two hours they reached their long awaited destination and drove them in.

"Well, that 'bout does it boys. I was sure sweatin' this one for sure. Mr. Knight, Javier, Carlos, muchas gracias! 'We couldn't a done it without you."

"No problem, Jake. Glad we could help out. That's what neighbors are for isn't it? Tell you what... I've got some business to take care of in town tomorrow but I'll send Javier and Carlos over to help with the brandin'."

"Mr. Knight, that would sure be kind of you. We could sure use the help."

"Good 'nough. Think I'll drop in and check up on Levi while I'm in there. Maybe they'll let me see the old coot. Well, adios boys it's been a hoot."

"Adios, vaqueros!"

Old man Knight and his cowboys rode toward the barn as Jake and his crew rode through the cattle giving them another once over before they called it a day.

The next morning the sun was coming up as Javier and Carlos pulled up to the barn. "Buenos dias hombres."

"Buenos dias, Senior Jake. We're ready to go. Senor Knight es goin'a shek up on Senor Lebi hoy."

Carlos chimed in. "Si. He want a make se-guro el doctore es doin' a goot yob."

"Mr Knight is a fine man! He and Dad go back a long ways."

Javier and Carlos led their horses as they walked toward the corrals to join up with Zeb and the boys.

"Buenos dias hombres," Zeb said. "Glad to see ya'."

"Buenos dias, Senor Zeb."

Tired from the previous day's work, Randy and Andy mounted their horses without saying a word. The crew rode into the branding trap to bring the cattle to the sorting alley. Soon they had them in the big corral next to the alley.

Jake said, "Zeb, go ahead and get the brandin' pot goin'. You boys get the vaccines and syringes, and we'll cut off the calves."

Javier rode into the calves and double hocked a calf, then headed to the branding pot. Randy and Andy grabbed the tight rope dragging the calf behind Javier's horse. Soon they had the calf flanked and secured, and removed Javiers' rope from the calf's back legs.

Jake reached down to cut the bawling calf. "Here we go again boys!"

Carlos was there with a hot iron and slapped it to the left hip of the calf. The familiar smell of singed hair and hide filled the smoky air.

"I swear I will *never* get used to that smell!"

"I know what you mean, Andy. It's some-thin' that stays with you for awhile that's for sure."

"You boys don't get too comfortable holdin' that calf down, we have plenty more to brand."

"Don't worry, Zeb, we'll stay up with you."

Javier built another loop and rode back into the calves, quickly double hocking one, and then headed to the flankers. One after another he con-tinued seldom missing.

"Darn, Randy! That Javier is wearin' me out! We no sooner get one branded an' he's here with another one!"

"I'm gettin' pretty spent too."

"It's been one of the hardest weeks of my life, with long days and worryin' about Granddad. Seems like one day just drifts into another. I can't separate the days anymore."

Jake headed toward another bull calf with his razor sharp knife and the can of smear. "You boys'll hold up. Just keep your mind on the work."

Carlos slapped a hot iron on the calf and Zeb hit him with 2 cc's of four way from the pistol syringe.

"You boys will live. Hell when I was your age I could flank calves all day and hit the honky tonks' 'till daybreak."

"Yeah, I'll bet!" Randy replied.

The day wore on as Javier dragged the last calf to the worn-out flanking crew.

"Well, boys, looks like we done it. We'll hold 'em in the trap tonight and scatter 'em in the Big

Brushy tomorrow. Andy, you and Randy throw them some of that cow hay."

"Okay, Dad. We'll get 'em taken care of soon as we unsaddle our horses."

"Thanks, Andy. Javier... Carlos, I sure want to thank you again for your help. Tell Mr. Knight thanks and I'll be over soon to see 'im."

Shaking Jake's hand, Javier said, "Bueno Senor Jake. We were berry hoppy to help."

"You boys better stay and have somethin' to eat before you head back." Jake said.

With broken Spanish-English, Javier said...Gracias Senior Yake ...pero no. Tenemos mas trabajo en el rancho hoy."

They shook Jakes hand and the two vaqueros turned and led their horses over to their trailer, loaded them and drove off.

Jake walked over to where Zeb was getting the branding pot and irons organized. "Well, that's the last of the brandin', except for any we may have missed."

"Yeah. Sure is a good feelin'. I don't think we missed many. Havin' Javier and Carlos helpn' made a lot of difference."

"That's for sure Zeb. They're damn good hands. Old man Knights' lucky to have those two!"

The crew finished up at the barn and headed for the house. As they walked through the door Andy said. "Boy somethin' sure smells good!"

"Yeah, smell those hot rolls! Wish my Mom could cook like that!"

Kathy smiled. "We knew you hard-working cowboys would need a good hot meal so Sally and I put one together."

Sally said, "Yep, you have a nice pot roast, beans, corn, hot rolls and sweet tea to wash it all down."

"Don't forget the desert."

"Oh yeah... apple pie."

Jake grinned. "See why I married her, boys? She's one of the best cooks in this part of Texas!"

They all sat down to the table. Kathy squeezed her husband's hand. "Jake would you give us a blessing?"

"Sure, Honey. We need to give the good Lord thanks for sure." He bowed his head. *"Lord, we want to thank you for helpn' us get our work done without anymore problems. We pray you will watch over Dad and help him to get better. We thank you for this fine meal and pray it will help keep us strong to do our work...Amen."*

"Amen" was repeated around the table.

"Honey, did you get in to check on Dad today?"

"Yes, we did. Samuel said the tests results came back. He wants to see us tomorrow and go over everything."

"Did he give you any idea of how he's doin'?"

"He didn't say all that much. He said he'd rather we be together when he gives us the results."

"Were you able to see Dad?"

"Yes, Sally and I went in to see him for a short time. He wasn't very coherent so we weren't able to visit."

Jake fell silent, a worried look came over his face as he stared into his plate, slowly swallowing his last bite. "Ya' know Samuel and I haven't been that close since he left the ranch. I know one thing about him though: if Dad wasn't in bad shape he'd a given you more information."

They all sat silently with worried expressions, trying to enjoy the fine meal.

"I think you and Kathy should head to the hospital first thing in the mornin'," Zeb said. "The boys and I can check the cattle and get 'em back to the Brushy."

"I appreciate that Zeb. We need to get the low down so we'll know what we're up against."

As they finished their last bite of apple pie the tired cowboys thanked Kathy and Sally Ann for the fine meal. Slowly they got up and headed for a warm shower and a much-needed nights sleep.

Chapter 9

"That Grullo sure is a pretty son of a gun Zeb."

"Yeah I've always liked these mousy lookin' horses."

"He's sure put together nice too. Looks like he could stop a freight-train."

"Tell you what, Randy... if you eat all your vegetables I might—just might—let you ride 'im sometime."

"I love vegetables, Zeb."

Zeb cracked a smile and nudged the Grullo in the side to move around the cattle in a trot.

"Boys, we better get these critters outta' here and back into the Brushy. Jake's countin' on us to finish up the job."

They bunched the cattle and headed them out.

"Come on, Sally, we need to get going."

"I know, Mom. I was just putting some of that apple pie in a container for Grandpa. I thought he might like some."

"I'm sure he would, Honey, but I'm not sure he'll be up to eating it."

Jake came into the house. "You gals 'bout ready to go?"

"Yes, we are. Sally's just fixing up a little treat for her Grandpa."

"What you got there?"

"Just a little of that apple pie we had left over."

"Tell you what... if he doesn't eat it I'll bet Sam would like it. Maybe we should take two pieces."

Sally hurried back into the kitchen cut another slice of apple pie, then headed out the door where her parents are patiently waiting in the car.

Jake,s jaws were clinched tightly as they headed down the dusty road.

Kathy put her hand on his arm. "Honey, I know you're terribly worried about your Dad. Please try to calm down a little. Things will be okay. I'm sure Samuel is doing everything he possibly can for Pop."

"I know, Honey. I just can't believe all this has happened! Dads' been such a strong individual all his life, he was one of the best calf ropers goin' down the road, he's taken care of the ranch and all of us through thick and thin, now he's laid up and no one seems to know what the outcome will be."

She squeezed his arm gently. "I know, Jake. We just have to be strong for him now. We can't let this get the best of us."

"You're right, as usual. We just have to hang and rattle."

The car moved along the highway like it was on automatic pilot. Jake's mind was a thousand miles away as he stared down the white line. It had been years since he'd experienced such fear. Years since the ambush that cost him the best buddy he had on his team. Now he faced the uncertainty that surrounded his mentor, the man who had guided him throughout his life.

He pulled into the hospital parking lot and quickly shut down the engine. "Well let's get in there!"

They hurried in and headed straight to the nurses' station. "Ma'am my name is Jake Blevins. We're lookin' for Doctor Samuel Blevins. He around?"

"Yes sir, he sure is. I'll page him for you."

She spoke into the handset "Paging Doctor Blevins... Paging Doctor Blevins... please come to the central nurses' station."

"Thank you Ma'm. We really appreciate your help."

After a few minutes Samuel came out and greeted his family "Good morning. I'm glad you could get in this early. How are things at the ranch?"

"Well thanks to Old Man Knight we finished up with the brandin'. He brought Javier and Carlos over and we gathered the Brushy. He had to come into town yesterday but sent his cowboys over to give us a hand."

Sam nodded. "He came by to see Dad, as a matter of fact. He didn't stay long, and Dad wasn't up to saying much. Let's go down to my office and visit a little before I take you to see him."

They quickly walked down to the office.

"Please have a seat. I know you're in a hurry to see Dad, but I need to discuss his condition with you."

"Well what's it look like, is he goin' to come out of it okay?"

"It's like this—Dad's left shoulder is broken and he has severe muscle, tendon and nerve damage. His left leg has a compound fracture and he has a concussion."

"Well, what have you done for him!"

"Hold on Jake. Calm down! We've surgically repaired his leg and it's looking good. We have to give him a couple of days rest before we go into the shoulder. The most critical problem we're faced with is neurological. He fractured a vertebrate in his neck and that's putting pressure on nerves."

"Okay, Sam... so how does that all add up?"

"The prognosis is uncertain with injuries like this. He could possibly have paralysis in his arms or legs... maybe both. We can't make that determination at this time."

"So what are his chances of bein' able to walk?"

"We just don't know, Jake. It could be weeks or months... or maybe never."

The room grew silent as Jake mulled the news around in his head.

"Sam, can we see Pop now?"

"Sure Kathy, but he's been sedated and he's on morphine to control the pain. He won't be coherent and he might not recognize any of us."

They left Samuel's office and headed to ICU.

"As I was saying earlier, Old Man Knight came by yesterday to see Dad. He just stood there and looked at him, and told him they had a lot of living to do so not to lay up too long. Then he turned and walked out. He didn't say much to me—just 'Adios and 'take good care of him.'"

They walked into Levi's room, Jake walked over by his Dad, fighting back his emotions as Kathy drew near, clutching his arm.

"Dad, we're here. We came to see you."

There was no response.

"Pop, we're here to see you."

"I guess he's too far under to recognize us. Maybe we should just let him rest."

Jake and Kathy turned to walk out as Sally Ann walked over to Levi's bedside. She set the container with the pie on his bed stand.

"Grandpa, I love you very much. Please come home soon." She clutched her handkerchief and the other a container of pie then turned around to walk out.

"Here, Uncle Samuel, this is for you."

"Thank you, Sally. That's awfully sweet of you!"

As they walked down the hall, Jake turned to his brother, his chest feeling like it was about to explode. "Well Brother thanks for being straight with us. I know it wasn't easy for you."

"I'll keep you posted on his progress. You just take care of yourself. Oh and if things are caught up at the ranch, Randy needs to get back to town. School's about to start and the swim and diving teams start their workouts next week."

Jake nodded. "I'll get him home. He's sure been a trooper out there. We really appreciate you and Verna lettin' him help us like you did. He's a hard worker for sure, just like Dad."

Jake turned to catch up with Kathy and Sally Ann, then paused and turned to see his brother watching him. "Gracias Hermano!"

"Por Nada Hermano!"

They climbed in the car and headed back to the ranch. It seemed to take forever to get there.

As they drove into the ranch Zeb was walking toward the house. They pulled up and got out.

"Glad you're back. How's he doin?"

"It's hard to say. Sam is being very cautious about his condition. Seems like he doesn't want to get our hopes up."

"Who would've ever thought this would happen to Levi. He's always been so damn tough!"

"I know what you mean, Zeb. He's always been the one takin' care of things."

"Jake if you don't mind I'd like to take a couple days off to sort things out a little."

"No problem. We can handle things around here now that the brandin's done. I'll get you some back pocket dinero while you get your plunder together."

"I'd appreciate that."

Zeb headed over to the bunkhouse as Jake went into the house to get some money out of the safe.

Chapter 10

"Here you go Zeb, this ought to keep you goin' for awhile."

"Thanks amigo. I hope you understand. I just need to clear my old cabeza a little."

Jake nodded. "I know how I'm feelin' right now with everything that's happened. I can only imagine what you're goin' through. Hell, you've known Dad longer than any of us. You just take whatever time you need. We'll take care of things out here."

"Thanks, Jake, I appreciate that." He got in his pickup and headed down the dusty road. Thoughts of the past week and the uncertainty surrounding his oldest friend weighed heavy on his mind.

The trip that normally seemed to take forever, passed quickly and the lights of the big city appeared out of the darkness like a bolt of lightning.

As he walked into the lobby a voice from behind the desk broke the silence. "What can I do for you, Sir?"

"I need a room for a couple of days."

"That's what we're here for. How many days will you be with us?"

"Just leave it open. I'm not sure."

The clerk quickly completed the transaction and Zeb headed to his room.

Hot water beating down on his tired back relieved the knots. Tension drained from his body, temporarily erasing his worries as he contemplated a night at the Lonely Bull.

"Howdy you old Geezer, where's your sidekick and those two cowboys?"

"Hola, Gordo. We had some tough luck at the ranch. Levi got busted up pretty bad and he's in the hospital."

"No Shit? What the hell happened?"

"His horse took a bad fall with him. It was a hell of a wreck! Purt'near killed him."

"Damn, I sure hate to hear that! Tell you what—put your dinero back in your pocket. There's no cover for you t'night."

"Thanks, Frank, I appreciate that. I just need to cool out a little."

As he walked over and sat down the Bunkhouse Boys are playing one of his old favorites *"Cowtown."*

"What'll it be cowboy?"

Zeb looked up to a familiar face. "I'll have a shot of rye with a Lone Star back."

As the well-endowed blond walked away he began to read the room and spotted a familiar face sitting alone across the dance floor: Ruth, one of the coeds.

"Here you go cowboy. rye, Lone Star back."

"Thanks, what do I owe ya'?"

"This ones on Frank."

He looked over and saw Frank standing at the end of the bar and held the shot of rye up. "Gracias amigo."

"Por nada, vaquero."

Sitting there nursing the spirits, Zeb continued watching Ruth sitting quietly deep in thought. Finally he picked up the long neck and walked over.

"Howdy, isn't your name Ruth?"

She looked up, startled out of her somber mood.

"Why yes. How—Oh, I remember... you were in here a couple days ago with your friend and two boys."

"Yeah and you were here with some of your friends from the university. Mind if I sit a spell?"

"Not at all, have a seat."

"How's the education goin'?"

"Not bad, I've finished all my semester finals and started on a thesis to complete my MBA."

"That sounds pretty intense."

"It's been nerve wracking, but I'm managing to do okay I guess. Where's your friend?"

"It's sorta' a long story. His horse took a bad fall with him while we were gatherin' cattle."

"Is he okay?"

"Not really. It was a pretty bad wreck and he's broke up pretty bad."

"That's just awful!"

"It really has me frazzled. We've been com-padres for quite a spell. I had to get away from the ranch for awhile to sort things out a little."

On her rounds the waitress stopped. "You two doin' okay?"

"Maybe you better bring us a couple," Zeb said, then looked at Ruth. "What you drinkin', Ruth?"

"Crown neat."

"Bring her a Crown. I'll have another rye."

"Thanks, Zeb. I could use another drink."

"You seem troubled. What's goin' on, if you don't mind me askin'?"

"I'm just worried about completing my MBA and concerned about what I'll do when I fin-ish it. The job market isn't all that great right now with the economy in the shape it's in."

"Ya' know, I've always found that things'll work themselves out in time. We just have to work a little harder at keepin' our minds on the big pic-ture. Right now there's some pretty good music and plenty of Crown. Maybe you just need to let things ride for awhile."

"You're right. It's time to relax and enjoy the night!"

Zeb held up his shot. "Here's mud in your eye!" She cracked a smile as they tipped their glasses.

"How 'bout a spin around the floor?"

As they danced to one song and then an-other, a warm glow of understanding came over them and he drew her closer. No words were spoken as they looked into each others eyes. The needs of two lonely people overtook them as they turned and walked toward the door, where Frank and the shapely waitress were standing.

"Where are you two headed?"

They just smiled at Frank and walked through the door.

The waitress said, "Well what do you think about that?"

Frank smiled. "It gives me hope."

Arm and arm Zeb and Ruth slowly walked into the dimly lit parking lot.

Back at the ranch, Jake looked at Kathy. "Wonder how Zeb's gettin' along?"

"Honey, he has really been worried about your Dad. I'm sure he's trying to get it all sorted."

Jake took a swallow of coffee. "Yeah... he and Dad have been through a lot together. They're more like brothers. Hell, I wish Sam and I were as close as those two."

He looked at the floor and shook his head. "Ya' know, it's really a shame that Sam can't stop blaming Dad and the ranch for Mom's death. God knows it almost killed Dad when she died. If it hadn't been for Zeb there's no tellin' what would have happened. Sam and I sure weren't old enough to be much help to him."

"It must have really been a shock for Pop. He loved her more than anything on this earth. I'll tell you one thing for sure though: Sam sure has taken this accident seriously. He's doing all he possibly can for your Dad, and he's trying to comfort all of us at the same time. That can't be easy for him after everything that's happened over the years."

Jake paused while taking another sip from the mug. "You're right I'm sure, he's probably trying to sort a lot out in his own mind. It can't be easy for him seeing Dad in that condition and unable to do much for him right now." He tipped his cup, finishing his coffee,and sat the cup on the table. "I think I'll get Andy and put out some salt. We need to spend some time together."

"Good idea, Honey. Sally and I'll have a nice dinner for you when you get back."

Jake got up walked to the sink, rinsed out his mug and put it in the sink, then turned back to Kathy and hugged her. "Thanks, sweetheart. I sure love you!"

He turned and headed out the door.

"I love you Jake, with all my heart!"

The jeep bounced up the rocky road as Jake and Andy held on tight. "Boy, Dad, this is barely a road. When it gets dry like this it seems like every rock gets uncovered."

"Before we got this old Jeep we had to pack salt out here on mules. That was a hell of a job."

He downshifted the Jeep. "This cow trail road doesn't bother me a bit."

He glanced out across the pasture, and pointed,excited. "Look Andy! You see that big buck over there?"

"Yeah! He's a big 'un for sure."

"Bout a five pointer. Maybe we better look him up sometime. We could use some venison."

They both watched as the buck bounded into a mesquite-covered arroyo.

"Damn, I love it out here!"

Chapter 11

The morning chores completed, Jake walked back to the house. In the distance he spotted Zeb's pickup headed toward the ranch. Kathy walked out on the front porch to see who was driving in.

"Looks like the drifter has come home."

"Sure does," Kathy said. "Your breakfast is ready."

"Thanks Honey, I'll be right there."

Zeb shut off the engine and walked over and shook Jake's hand. "Well, it's good to have you back," Jake said. "We missed ya'. How'd it go?"

"Went pretty well. I had time to think a few things over and clear up some problems I was dealin' with. Sometimes a man just needs time to reflect on things."

"Well I'm glad you had a good time. Come in and tell us all about it."

"I cain't tell you the whole story. It gets sort'a personal."

"Damn Zeb, that sounds downright interestin'! Maybe we better save some of your story for another time."

"Mebbe I'd better keep it to myself. Sometimes it's better not to give up all your secrets!"

They walked into the kitchen.

Kathy smiled. "Morning, Zeb. Nice to have you back. How were things in town?"

"Ah, you know how it is... not much goin' on in there, just the same old sixes and sevens."

"How about some breakfast?"

"No thanks Kathy I ate 'fore I left town. Coffee'll do for now. Any news 'bout Levi?"

Jake shook his head. "No, nothing over the weekend. Sam's supposed to call us today sometime and give us an update."

"We'll be goin' into town today anyway to check on 'im"

"Did the kids start back to school?"

"Yes, they went back today, under protest. They wanted to go into town and see their Grandpa."

"Guess Randy went back to town too."

"Yeah... you know how Sam and Verna are. They don't want him out here anymore than possible."

"That's a shame! That boy loves ranchin', an' he's so much like Levi it ain't funny."

"He's a pistol alright. Looks like he'll be on the varsity divin' team this year."

The phone rang and Kathy walked over to answer it.

"Hello? Hi Sam, we were just talking about you. How's Levi?

Oh...okay, I'll tell Jake. Thanks, Sam. Goodbye." She hung up and looked at Jake.

"Honey, that was Sam. He said Pop was coherent, but very confused. He's asking about everyone."

"Hell, we'd better get to town!"

"Mind if I ride along?"

"Why hell no! He'd be madder n' hell if you weren't there."

The men hurriedly cleaned off the table.

Kathy said, "Just put those in the sink. I'll wash them up when we get back."

"We'll take the dualie. I have some things to pick up in town."

They made a quick trip into the hospital, looking forward to news about Levi.

Samuel was at the nurse's station when they walked in. "Good morning. It's good to see all of you again."

"Thanks for the call. How's he doin'?"

"He seems to be doing better. He's still on pain medication, but his alertness has improved. He's been asking about things at the ranch."

"Did you tell 'em we finished with the brandin'?"

Sam grinned. "Yes, that seemed to be his main concern. He was more worried about that than his own condition."

Zeb shook his head. "Knowin' Levi that figures."

"Let's go into my office and I'll give you a rundown on his treatments."

In the office, Sam motioned to the chairs. "Please, have seat."

Kathy said, "Will we be able to see him?"

Sam nodded. "Yes. Just let me go over a few things with you first. As you know we surgically repaired his leg. It was a very severe fracture. We used splints made from a new compound. We're having better results with it rather than the stainless splints."

Jake asked. "How long will he have them?"

"Probably for the rest of his life. Unfortunately at this stage of his life the bones probably won't heal to the point the splints can be removed. We have found on younger patients it is sometimes possible to remove them after time."

"I'll bet that'll keep him laid up for awhile."

"Unfortunately, Zeb your probably right. He'll be in a wheelchair for awhile, then a walker until he regains the strength in his leg."

"That's only part of his overall condition. His left shoulder was fractured and he has a great deal of tendon and muscle damage."

"So what do you do for that?" Jake asked.

"It'll take additional surgeries to repair the damage and there's no guarantee on the outcome. These injuries are complicated due to their severity and the amount of nerve damage that has occurred...He'll probably experience mobility problems."

"My gosh! Will he be able to use his arm?"

"We'll have a better understanding once the surgeries are completed."

Jake's voice quivered. "How long will all of this take?"

"He's scheduled for surgery on his shoulder in the morning. If all goes well he should be stable enough in two weeks to address any further nerve damage. I know this all sounds very complicated to all of you, but believe me, I will do everything I can for him! Again,these are not simple injuries we are dealing with and at his age we have to take it one step at a time. Rushing things could cause serious complications."

Kathy asked,"Can we see him now, Samuel?"

"Sure Kathy. I'll take you to his room."

Samuel led them into Levi's room. "Look whose come to see you, Dad."

"Bout damn time you showed up! What's goin' on at the ranch? Brandin' done?"

"Calm down, Dad, Jake will fill you in on things."

Kathy smiled. "Hello Pop, it's sure good to see you."

"Oh Kathy, forgive me I didn't recognize you when you came in. God bless you for comin' to see me."

"Howdy, Dad how you feelin?"

"I've been better. How's things goin' at the ranch?"

"It's goin' well, Dad. Thanks to Mr. Knight we got the brandin' done. We're just waitin' on you to get back and line us out."

Zeb grinned. "Yeah, your layin' 'round in here ain't helpin' things at all."

"Zeb you old coot. What the hell you been up to? Chasin' any wild heifers' lately?"

"Nah, just sorta mindin' my p's an' q's. You know how it is...the ranch takes up most of the day."

"Dad we better let you get some rest. You have a long day ahead of you tomorrow. Everyone wants you back on your feet and out of here as soon as possible. Besides, Randy has some diving meets coming up pretty soon and he wants you there to watch him."

"Yeah Dad, you know how Randy is. He'd be plumb let down if you weren't there. You just rest and heal up."

"Pop, you mind Samuel. We want you home with us as soon as possible. We love you and miss you."

"Thanks Sweetie. I'll get there quick as I can."

Zeb walked over looked down at Levi. "See you later, amigo."

Levi turned his head and faced the back wall as his family left.

"What you think, Sam?"

"I'll know better after the surgery tomorrow.

Hopefully he'll be strong enough to start occupational therapy in a couple of days and then some light physical therapy in a couple of weeks after that. It just depends on how he comes out of the surgery."

"Any idea when he might come home?"

"There's no way of telling right now...perhaps three or four weeks...I just don't know. Like I've been saying, we'll have a better idea once we complete the surgeries."

Reaching the hospital exit, Jake turned to say goodbye to Samuel.

"Sam thanks again for givin' it to us straight. We really appreciate what your doin' for Dad."

"You don't have to thank me. I love him too, despite our differences. He's strong willed and tough as an old boot, and that will be to his advantage during his recovery."

Kathy walked over to Samuel and kissed him on the cheek. "Thanks again, Sam. please keep us informed of his progress."

"Rest assured I will."

Zeb grinned. "Y'know, I wondered what it was goin' to take to get y'all talkin' again. This hasn't been one of my better experiences in life but hopefully it will bring about good things. Take care of my old compadre. We have lots to do yet."

"Don't you worry, Zeb, we're doing everything we possibly can and then some."

Samuel waved to them as they drove out of the parking lot, his chest full of emotions he hasn't felt in years.

Chapter 12

"Thanks, Sam. I appreciate the update."

"Who was that Honey?"

"It was Sam. they've completed the surgery on Dad's shoulder."

"Did he say how it went?"

"He said that the surgery went well, but when they got into the shoulder the muscle and tendons had been damaged to the point that there was very little they could put back together. They also had to remove bone that had been broken lose. They hope he'll be stable enough in a few days to begin some occupational therapy."

"Did he say when we would be able to see him?"

"No, he didn't say, but I'm sure Dad won't be very coherent for a day or so. We might as well just wait 'till Sam tells us we can come in to see him. He'll call us I'm sure."

"I'm goin' to get Zeb and ride out to the Big Brushy and check those calves again, make sure they're pickin' up okay."

"I've got plenty of catching up to do around here. We've been gone so much my house work is falling behind."

Jake gave his sweet lady a hug and peck on the cheek. "We'll be back later."

"You two be careful out there."

"Don't worry. We will be, for sure."

As he approached the corral he spotted Zeb working with a three year old. "That's sure enough a nice lookin' gray."

"Sure is. He'll make a good one if he keeps goin' like he is. He learns quick and doesn't forget much. A few days more of ground work and I'm gonna take him over to Javier to start ridin'."

"That sounds good to me. That vaquero can sure do wonders with a colt."

"One of the best I ever saw. What you got on your mind?"

"Thought we'd ride out to the Brushy and ride through those calves."

"Good idea. I'll catch up a couple horses."

"Thanks, Zeb."

As the noonday sun passed overhead the cowboys had made a wide circle through the Big Brushy.

"The calves are doin' pretty damn good."

Zeb comments. "Yeah, I'm surprised, as dry as its' been. I haven't seen it this bad since '68."

"It was plenty wet where I was in '68."

"Yeah, I'll bet it was."

Jake looked into an arroyo. "Look there. Let's get down there!"

The two cowboys eased their way into the deep arroyo and rode to what appeared to be a dead calf.

As they rode closer the buckskin snorted and pointed his ears.

"Hell, that calf looks like a lion got 'im!"

Jake got off the buckskin and led him closer to the dead calf, and tried to get a better look.

"Yeah, looks like a big cat got 'im. Look at those tracks!"

"Hell, Jake he's got paws big as a pie pan! I Haven't seen anything like that in years. That son of a bitch must'a drifted in here from along ways off."

"Sure enough. He won't quit this shit either. We'll need to get D.C. in here with his lion dogs. I'll call 'im when we get back."

It was late afternoon by the time they rode in. They quickly unsaddled their horses.

"I'll take care of things here, if you need to call D.C."

"Thanks, I'd better get him out here pronto or we'll be losin' more cattle."

Zeb said. "That's for damn sure."

"Hello D.C. This is Jake Blevins. How you doin' this evenin' Sir? That sounds good. What I'm callin' 'bout is we found a dead calf today. Looked like a cat got it. Yeah that's what we thought too. We were wonderin' if you could bring your dogs over. That sounds great!"

Jake hung up and walked back to the barn where Zeb was feeding horses and pitching hay to a doggie calf.

"I got hold of him. He'll be out in the mornin'."

The men heard baying hounds as D.C.'s truck pulled into the ranch and came to a stop at the barn.

A burley six-foot-four man stepped out of the pickup and walked over to where Jake and Zeb were standing.

"Mornin,' boys. How's it goin'?"

"Pretty good Sir, considering the problem we're havin' with that cat." Jake said.

"I'm sure we can handle that little problem for you."

D.C. unloaded his horse from the trailer, then released the hounds from the pen in the bed of the truck.

The Blue Tick hounds followed along as they rode away from the barn headed for the Big Brushy. Shortly they approached the area where Jake and Zeb had found the dead calf the day before. The hounds began to pick up the scent of the predator as they slowly worked their way into the arroyo. They tilted their heads upward as they neared the dried blood where the calf had taken its last breath. D.C. sensed a problem, then quickly dismounted and snapped a long chain on both the dogs.

Jake said, "Hell, it's gone!"

"That doesn't surprise me. That cat didn't go far after it made the kill. It was probably watchin' you boys when you came up on the calf". He pointed up the arroyo. "She drug him off that way."

The hunting party followed the trail, D.C. holding tightly to the hounds as they came upon the mutilated carcass. "There's what's left."

"Damn, that cat ate most of him"

"Boys, I'm thinkn' that cat's not by itself. See those tracks? Looks like a couple of cubs."

"What'll we do now D.C.?"

"This is gonna be a bit more complicated than I was countin' on. I think we'd better call in the Game Department. They'll send out a team to tranquilize all of 'em and haul 'em outta here. That momma cat's probably up there in those out-crops. She ain't goin' far from all the feed you're providin' 'er. Let's get back and I'll give the de-partment a call. Maybe they can get a team out here tomorrow."

"Sounds good to me. We'll do whatever you think's best. You're the pro."

D.C. nodded. "Don't know about the pro. part, but I've been doin' this for a long time and I can read sign pretty well. I'll stay at the ranch to-night if they can get out here in the mornin', if it's okay with you."

"No problem, D.C.. We'd be glad to have your company."

Quickly as they could they made their way back to headquarters.

"I'll get my dogs tended to and make the call."

"Thanks, D.C.. We'll take care of your horse."

When D.C. came in, he picked up the phone and dialed. "Hello... yeah this is D.C. Williams. I need to speak to Jerry." He paused, waiting for the other man to get on the line. "Afternoon, Jerry this is D.C.. Got a situation out here at the Blevin's ranch. A big female cat killed a calf, and it looks like she has a cub or two. Yeah, we found where she'd killed it and drug it off. There were tracks that looked like cubs'. That would be great, Jerry. We'll see you in the mornin'."

He hung up the phone as the others walked in.

"Did you get hold of 'im?"

"Yeah, sure did. Jerry and a couple of his men will be here first thing in the mornin'. They'll bring out one of them big cages on their 4x4. After what I saw today I don't think we'll have a problem findin' that cat. Those fish and game boys work pretty fast once they locate one. They'll tranquilize 'em and get 'em outta here pronto."

Zeb asked. "What'll they do with em?"

"Hard to say they may send 'em to a zoo. It's in their hands once they capture 'em. For sure they'll tag 'em, and sometimes they put a monitoring device on 'em."

Jake said. "I don't care what they do with 'em as long as they don't come back."

"Don't think you'll have to worry 'bout that. They won't be anywhere near here when they release 'em."

Things were ready for the hunt when the men from the game department drove in. D.C. walked over as they got out of their 4x4.

"Mornin', Jerry. Who you got here with you?"

"You remember Jack and Clayton don't you?"

"Oh hell yes. How you boys doin'?–Fellas, I'd like you to meet Jake Blevins and Zeb Pike." D.C. hesitated. "Is this little Andy?"

"Yes it is, D.C.. I figured maybe he might learn somethin' today that he wouldn't learn at school."

"You can probably take that to the bank for sure."

One of the men offered his hand. "Howdy. I'm Jerry Poole and this is Jack Tibbs and Clayton White."

Jake shook his hand. "We're pleased to meet you."

"We better get on the trail. Don't want you to lose anymore calves. What's the best way to get in there?"

"There's a cow trail road that runs up along that hog back. It leads over close to that outcrop where D.C. figured that cat's hangin' out. We can lead you in there on horseback."

They set out slowly, leading the 4x4 up the narrow road. The going was slow as they bounced from one rock to another.

D.C. had his hounds tightly controlled as they reached the top of the hog back and worked their way to the outcrop.

"This is 'bout as far as we can go with that vehicle."

They watched as the team from the game department prepared their equipment and readied their tranquilizer rifles. D.C. led the way with his hounds. As they drew closer to the outcrop, the hounds let out the familiar baying and lunged forward, hitting the end of the chains. It was all D.C. could do to hold them back.

"Y'all ready?"

"Sure are D.C., let 'em go."

D.C. reached down and struggled to release the hounds, who picked up the scent and raced toward the rough outcrop as D.C. and the government team struggled to keep up in the rocky terrain.

The dogs reached a rough undercut ledge and began baying louder. Then came the ferocious scream of an enraged cougar.

"There she is, Jerry!"

"Sure is. She's got those cubs backed into that undercut behind her trying to protect them."

The Blue Ticks' bayed and held her in the undercut as Jack moved up beside Jerry. "I think I can get a dart in her from here."

"Give it a shot!"

Jack took careful aim and fired the tranquilizer dart at the big cat, hitting her in the hip. She jumped straight in the air, forgetting the baying hounds as she tried to break and run, but the potent solution dulled her senses and she fell to the ground. The cubs trotted over to her and began to sniff her as they pawed at her motionless body. D.C. and Jake grabbed the collars and secured the hounds before they could give chase.

"We'd better get those cubs sedated."

"Go ahead Clayton."

The men quickly tied the legs of the mother cougar and her cubs. A couple of the men quickly placed a long pole between the cougar's tethered legs and lifted her, carrying her toward their vehicle. Others' carried the cubs. They secured the three cats in the cage.

Andy grinned. "Wow that was excitin' for sure!"

Jake said. "Sure was Andy. I been to two goat ropin's and a county fair and I ain't never seen nothin' like that!"

"I told you those boys work fast."

"That's an understatement, D.C.."

"If you fellas don't mind we'll go ahead and get outta here. We need to get this little family back to the compound as quick as we can."

Jake shook his hand. "Go ahead, Jerry. Do what you gotta do. We'll check cattle as we head back."

D.C looked at Jake. "Mind if me and the dogs tag along with you? I'd like to see more of the country."

"No problem, D.C.. You're more than welcome after all you've done for us."

As they headed out of the Big Brushy the hounds followed behind, just another day on the trail for them.

"Good morning, Mr. Blevins. Ready for a little occupational therapy this morning?"

"What's this Mr. Blevins crap? I'm your Dad. Damn it anyway, Samuel I've 'bout had all this bullshit I can handle. Occupational therapy. What the hell is that? I'm a rancher for Christ's sake! I don't need no one tellin' me how to be a cowboy."

"Calm down, Dad, it's not as bad as you're thinking. We just want to check your motor skills and make sure you can handle normal activities."

An orderly entered the room with a wheelchair. "Are we ready?"

"'Bout as ready as can be expected I guess."

The orderly assisted Levi into the wheelchair and wheeled him out.

"Good morning folks. My name's Janet. I'll be working with you for a couple of days, assessing your normal daily activities. Before we get started are there any questions?"

Levi held up his good arm.

"Is it Mr. Blevins?"

"Yes, Ma'am."

"What is your question, Sir?"

"I don't see any horses or cattle in here. How am I goin' to work at my normal daily activities?"

Janet chuckled. "Mr. Blevins, we're not quite that advanced here yet. We'll just be helping you with your personal activities, such as using a toothbrush, washing, and combing your hair. We'll also observe how well you use your silverware and other tasks you sometimes take for granted."

Over the next hour the group set about performing prescribed activities as the therapist observed and took notes. After a couple of hours, Janet said. "Thank you, folks. That will be all for today. The orderlies will return you to your rooms now, and I'll see you in the morning."

While making his rounds, Samuel dropped in to see his father. "How'd it go, Dad?"

"I've had more meaningful days. What's with this crap anyway?"

"Bear with it. We just want to make sure you can handle basic activities. Once we're satisfied with your progress you'll move on to more intense physical therapy. Actually, the therapist thought you did quite well for your first day. You'll be through this before you know it."

"When will I go back to the ranch?"

"Dad, just be patient. We'll get you home as soon as we can. I'll give Jake a call and let him know how you're doing."

Jake answered his phone. "Hello? Howdy, Sam. How are things goin'? I'll bet that was somethin' to watch. I'm glad to hear he's up and movin'. We've had some excitement out here for sure. A big female cat fed her two cubs on a calf over in the Big Brushy, an' it turned into a two-day hunt. Nah we didn't kill 'em. Old D.C. came over with his hounds and found 'em and called in the game department. They sent a team in that tranquilized 'em and hauled 'em outta here, thank God. We checked more of the cattle an' didn't find anymore dead ones, so I guess that calf filled 'em up. Sure we'll be in tomorrow mornin'. Hey, don't tell Dad 'bout the calf. It'll just get him riled up. Okay Sam, we'll see you tomorrow. Adios."

Chapter 13

It's mid-morning. Sam had just completed his rounds and was finishing some reports when he heard a knock at his door.

"Come In." — He glanced up as Jake and Kathy walked in.

"Good mornin', Sam."

"Please excuse my laziness. I was working on these reports and thought you might be one of the nurses. How are you two today?"

"Actually things seem to be goin' pretty well. We finished up with things at the ranch this mornin' in fairly good time and figured we'd better get in here to see Dad."

Kathy asked, "How's he doing, Sam?"

"Actually, he looks a great deal better, and he's coming along with the occupational therapy. I think he'll start physical therapy on Monday."

"Wow, that's encouraging!"

"How's the lion hunting going? That's really something that you found a lion out there. Bet it was quite an adventure."

"It sure wasn't a normal couple days, that's for sure. We were pretty worried 'till they got 'em caught."

"You say there was a female and two cubs?"

"Yeah, they were cute little things but their momma was a ferocious actin' bitch for sure. I think those fish and game boys took 'em over to their compound where they band 'em and give 'em the once over. They may even put some kind of electronic trackin' device on 'em."

"That's exciting stuff."

"Wasn't too excitin' for that calf."

"What's Pop up to right now Samuel?"

"He'll be in therapy for another hour, and then they'll take him back to his room and we can go see him."

Jake asked. "Randy doin' okay?"

"Why yes he is. He's back in school and going to diving practice. I think they're going to have some practice meets in a couple weeks or so. About four schools get together at the university and compete. It's pretty much like a regular meet, but the points don't count for season-end awards. Randy takes it just as serious though."

"I'm sure he does. At the ranch, he takes everything serious, watchin' him and Dad together was like watchin' everything in stereo. He's so much like him it isn't funny."

"I know what you mean. When I ask him something it's like listening to Dad when he answers they sound so much alike."

"It's spooky for sure."

"How're Andy and Sally Ann doing?"

"They're both doin' well, thank you for askin'. The other day when we went out after that lion I kept Andy home from school so he could tag along. He's still talkin' 'bout it."

"I bet he is."

"How's Verna doing, Samuel?"

"That's a good question. I haven't seen much of her with everything I have going on around this place. I'm here about seventy hours a week."

There's a knock at the door. "Yes?"

It was a nurse. "Doctor they've taken Mr. Blevins back to his room."

"Thank you." He looked at Jake and Kathy.

"Would you like to go down and see him now?"

"Oh yes we sure would!"

In the room, Levi glanced toward the door. "Well I'll be damned. Look who's here."

"Howdy Pop." Kathy walked over and gave him a kiss on the forehead.

"You're the sweetest thing around this place. It's sure good to see you Honey!"

"Howdy Dad."

"How's things at the ranch?"

"It's been goin' pretty well. Nothin' too outta the ordinary."

"What's Zeb up to these days?"

"He's been ridin' the pastures a lot and workin' with some of the colts. He's got a couple ready to take over to Javier to ride."

"That sounds good. He used to ride 'em pretty damn good too. Guess he's gettin' a little long in the tooth to do much of that anymore."

"The therapist told me your therapy is coming along well, Dad. You'll be ready to start physical therapy on Monday."

"I'm glad to hear that. The sooner the better. I want to get out of this place. I need some of Kathy's cookin' for a change. You don't know how well you got it till you're stuck in a place like this."

"Thanks, Pop. You really know how to make a girl feel special."

"Only one other gal that I know could cook like you and that was my Rita. She could make an old leather sole taste good."

"Is there anything we can bring you?"

"If you could bring Jose Cuervo by to visit. I'd like to see 'im."

Samuel said, "Dad, you know that's not possible. With the medication you're taking it could create more problems than we need right now."

Levi winked at Kathy. "Isn't that just like a doctor to shoot down a great idea?"

"Come on now Dad. I just want you to heal up so you can get out of here. Besides, Randy is looking forward to you coming to some of the diving meets he's got lined up."

"I wouldn't want to do somethin' that would keep me from goin' to those for sure."

"Well then just keep up your momentum in therapy and don't be asking for Senior Cuervo, and everything should turn out like you want it to."

Jake piped in. "Yeah Dad. We need you back at the ranch. We have a bunch of fence to build and we need all the hands we can get."

"That'll be the day."

A nurse came in. "I hate to break up this party, but his lunch is on its way. He needs to wash up and get ready to eat."

"Listen, I sure appreciate y'all droppin' in. Tell Zeb to come by if he gets in to town."

"We sure will."

"Pop you behave yourself."

They walked out as the orderly brought in a tray.

Jake said, "That's the best he's looked in quite awhile."

Samuel answered. "Yes he's improving. But the problem he's having with his shoulder is extremely serious. Tendons and muscle that are damaged as bad as his were, just don't heal well...much less the nerve damage that's causing the partial paralysis."

"Is there anyway we can help him?"

"I'm afraid it's out of our hands at this point. All we can do is try to improve things with therapy and pray he can overcome some of the problems he's having."

Jake grew silent as he stared down the hallway. "Somethin's got to turn this nightmare around. He just can't go out like this. He's been too strong all his life."

"We're doing all we can, Brother believe me, I don't want to see this continue either."

Kathy said, "We know you are Samuel, and we love you for all your doing for Pop."

"We'd better get goin'. I need to pick up some things at the feed store."

"Let us know how he's getting along," Kathy said.

"Don't worry. You'll be the first to know of any change whatsoever."

"Thanks Hermano."

They drove into the ranch with Levi's condition heavy on their minds.

"Honey, I'm gonna' let you out at the house. I need to take that box of shoes we picked up down to the barn."

"Sure, Honey. I need to start dinner, and the kids will be getting home from school pretty soon."

As he carried the box of horseshoes into the barn, Zeb was working on Levi's saddle.

"What you doin,' Zeb?"

"Figured I'd better get this saddle restrung. Levi'll be gettin' outta the horsepistol pretty soon and he's gonna' need it. How's he doin' anyway?"

"Sam said they were goin' to start him on physical therapy next Monday. Hopefully he'll pick up and they'll let 'im out pretty soon. Let's hope he'll be needin' that saddle."

"Ya think it would put you behind if I went into town over the weekend?"

"Hell no. You head on in if you want to. Dad asked me to tell you to come by if you ever got into town, I know he misses you."

"I was hopin' he was up to seein' me. I really miss talkin' to him. I'll work a little more on this saddle then head in."

"No problemo, amigo. You need any dinero?"

"Nah, I think I got it handled okay."

"Well if you do let me know!"

"Thanks amigo I appreciate that."

Zeb continued to work on the saddle, thinking about another night at the Lonely Bull, and hoping he might run into Ruth again.

Jake walked back into the house.

"What took you so long?"

"Oh Zeb and I were just talkin' a little. He's re-stringin' Dad's saddle. He's figurin' Dad will need it when he gets home and he doesn't want him to see it in the shape it's in."

"He said he's goin' into town over the weekend, an' he wants to go by and see Dad. I think he might have somethin' goin' over at the Lonely Bull too."

"Really? Has he said something to you?"

"No... it's just a hunch I have after the last time he went into town. He wasn't actin' himself when he came back, he was walkin' 'round like a February Stud."

"Sounds like him pullin' out now."

Jake walked over to the front door as Zeb drove toward town. "Looks like he's in a hurry. He's beginin' to act like a teenager."

Zeb walked through the door of the Lonely Bull. "Howdy Frank!"

"Well, I'll be damned! You're back for another go-round, are you? That little gal Ruth's been in askin' about you."

"She has?"

"Matter of fact she just came in about half-hour ago. She's sittin' at her usual table. How's Levi gettin' along?"

Paying very little attention to Frank, Jake fumbled in his pocket for the cover. "Oh he's comin' along."

He handed him the cover charge and walked over to Ruth. "Howdy!"

She looked up at the lanky old cowboy. "Why hello there stranger. Where have you been hiding?"

"Ah you know, just workin' out at the ranch. We've had a little excitement."

"Y'all seem to always have some excitement going on out there. Sit down and tell me about it."

As he sat, the familiar, well-endowed blond waitress walked up. "What'll it be cowboy? Your usual?"

"Yeah, a shot of rye and Lone Star back, and bring her another Crown neat."

"Thanks, I appreciate that."

"No problema."

"Well tell me. What happened now?"

"Oh, Jake and me were checkin' some of the calves we'd branded and found a dead'n a lion had killed."

He continued with the story as the waitress walked up. "Here you go folks. Enjoy."

Jake threw a ten spot on her tray. "Thanks, keep the change."

Ruth said, "Wow, you have had some excitement out there. I'd love to see the place sometime."

"Do you ride?"

"Doesn't every gal in these parts ride?"

"Guess that was a stupid question."

"My Dad was an avid polo player, and he started all of us out pretty early. All of us had horses and we'd ride every chance we got."

"That musta' been alright. You'll have to come out sometime. We've got some pretty good caballos out there. None of 'em ever played polo, but they're pretty damn good cowhorses."

"I'll bet they are."

"Ya' say your Dad used to play polo. Doesn't he play anymore?"

"No, he had a heart attack two years ago and it... it took him."

"I'm sorry to hear that, Ruth."

"It was pretty hard on us for a while. He was such a powerful man both in stature and in business."

"What sort' a business was he in?"

"He was a stock broker. He invested mainly in oil and electronics. He got the oil bug from Granddad, who was a wildcatter."

"You sure have an interestin' family."

"They're a hoot alright. My brother sort' a took things over after Dad died. He's in the same office in Houston."

Zeb saw Ruth was becoming stressed as she talked about her family. "How'd you like to dance?"

She smiled, "Thanks. I thought you'd never ask."

He pulled her close as the Bunkhouse Boys played *"Waltz Across Texas."*

Zeb grinned. "They sure can handle a waltz."

"So can you, Mr. Pike."

He held her even tighter as she pressed her trim body closer. They moved together as one, never missing a step; she sighed with disappointment as the waltz came to an end.

"That was wonderful, I truly love to waltz, specially with a cowboy who knows his way around the dance floor."

"That's sweet of you to say. Maybe we can get another one in before the night's up."

She squeezed his hand tightly as they made their way back to the table.

Ruth asked, "How's Levi doing?"

"He seems to be improving somewhat. He's goin' through some sort of therapy. Still cain't walk,though. They pushed him around in a damned wheelchair." A pained expression crossed his face as he spoke of his life-long compadre.

"Do you think he'd mind if I went to see him?"

"He'd be tickled pink if you dropped in on 'im. Hey, I'm goin' to see him tomorrow. How'd you like to go with me?"

"I'd love to!"

Zeb held up the shot of rye. "It's a date then."

Ruth smiled as she acknowledged the toast. "It's a date."

The Bunkhouse Boys began to play an old Haggard tune. *"Today I Started Loving You Again."* Zeb and Ruth looked at each other as they walked to the dance floor.

He pulled her close, feeling her warm breath on his neck as they danced. "How'd you like to get some coffee?"

"That sounds good, Zeb... I hope there's some in your room."

"Yep, there sure is, and the coffee shop puts out a pretty mean breakfast."

The couple walked hand in hand past Frank and out the front door.

"You two be gentle now."

Zeb grinned. "Always, my good friend... always!"

He watched them walk toward the pickup. "Damn I'm gonna' have to start drinkin' rye with Lone Star back!"

"What can I get for you folks?"

"What looks good to you, Gal?"

"Think I'll have the scrambled eggs with cheese, raisin toast with apple butter and grits."

"Sausage or Bacon?"

"Bacon, crisp please."

"I'll have two eggs over easy, sausage patties and hash browns."

"Anything else folks?'

"Guess that'll do for now."

Zeb looked at Ruth. "You really are a Southern Gal aren't ya'? Not many ladies order grits."

"Our family has been in Texas, since before it was a state. They fought at San Jacinto when Houston's boys captured Santa Anna, and Dad's third great grandfather was one of Hood's staff officers at Gettysburg."

"Your family has quite a history."

"Yes... some of it's not all that great. We've had a couple bad apples along the way."

Zeb chuckled. "Doesn't every family?"

She looked at him seriously.

"Zeb, I want you know that after our last night together, you were on my mind a great deal of the time. I was extremely excited when you walked in to the Lonely Bull last night. I could hardly sit still! You're such an interesting person. I'm so at ease and can say about anything I feel like saying when I'm with you."

"I'm glad that you feel that way. Bein' with you has brightened things up for me too. Ranchin's been my life since Levi and I got home from Europe, and it's all I know, but it get's damn lonely out there. : Spendin' the little time I have with you really has picked up my spirits. 'Specially after what's happened to Levi. Oh, and speakin' of Levi, we'd better get over to see 'im pretty soon. He'll sure be surprised to see you again, for sure."

At the hospital, they walked to the nurses station and Zeb inquired. "Ma'am, can you tell me what room Levi Blevins is in?"

"Yes Sir, he's on the second floor room fourteen. He's probably back from his morning therapy, so you can go on up."

Levi turned his head toward the door just as Zeb and Ruth walked in.

"Don't you think you should do something 'sides lay around all day?"

"Damn you!" 'Bout time you got in here to see me."

"I been here before. You were just too damned doped up to know I was here."

"Who's this you have with you?"

"You remember Ruth? She was at the Lonely Bull with her friends when we took the boys to town."

"Why hell yeah I remember! How you doin', Miss?"

"Very well, thank you for askin'."

"Well, if you two ain't a sight for sore eyes. What's goin' on out in the world?"

"Same ol' sixes and sevens. you know how it is."

"Sure do. Wish like hell I could get back out there. I'm 'bout to go nuts in here! They have me doin' some of the damndest things. It's getting to the point that every time I wipe my ass, they're takin' notes to see if I do it okay. Enough 'bout me–what's goin' on with you two?"

"Ah, we've been spendin' a little time together doin' some dancing and stuff out at the Bull."

Levi squints, as he looks at Zeb. "Sounds interesting."

"To be honest with you Levi, Zeb and I have had some very wonderful nights and breakfasts together too."

"Now we're gettin' down to the nut cuttin'! What's wrong with you Zeb? I was born at night, but not *last night*. Hell, I've known you too long."

"I know... I just sort'a didn't want to say anything outta turn."

"I'm a big girl." Ruth said. "You're not going to hurt my feelings. You should know that by now."

"I think it's down right intrestin', an' all I got to say is that you're one lucky son of a bitch. An' I mean that in a friendly way. You better treat this little lady well!"

"I'm doin' my best for sure."

Samuel walked in. "Hello, Zeb how are things going for you? Who's this you have with you?"

Levi grinned. "That's how he's doin'. Just look at that pretty little filly. Ain't she somethin'?"

Ruth held out her hand. "Hello, Doctor. I'm a friend of your dad's and this piece of jerky."

"Pleased to meet you Ma'am. Folks, I hate to break up this little get together, but I need to take a look at Dads' shoulder."

"No problem. We need to get goin' anyway.

It was nice seeing you, Levi. You get to feeling better. We need you at the ranch."

"I'm doin' my best."

"It was a pleasure meeting you, Dr. Blevins."

"Just call me Sam. That's what these two do."

"Okay, Sam. It sure was nice meeting you."

The two turned and walked down the hallway.

"Whaddya think of that, Sam? That old fart really gathered a looker!"

"He sure did. I may have to write a prescription for some of those blue tablets for him."

Levi grinned. "Yeah. Sure hope he doesn't blow a valve."

Chapter 14

"Good morning Mr. Blevins."

"Mornin' Ma'am, guess you're here to get me started on that physical therapy."

"Yes Sir. The sooner we get started the sooner you'll be able to go home."

Sam walked in. "Good morning everyone... sorry I'm a little tardy."

"Not a problem, Doctor, your Dad and I were just discussing the plans we have to get him out of here as quickly as possible."

"Yeah Sam, she was sayin' if things went well I might be able to get back to the ranch next week."

"We'll see how it goes, Dad. You realize you'll have to continue your therapy and return a couple times a week to monitor your progress."

"Whatever—just as long as I can get back to the ranch!"

"Mr. Blevins, we'll start you out with some light shoulder exercises. Then we'll progress to water therapy, and other advanced treatment as warranted."

"What's water therapy?"

"You'll be lifted into the pool with a mechanical lift chair. A therapist will assist you in the pool with leg exercises to improve strength and mobility. Don't worry. We'll be watching you closely."

"Do you have any other questions Dad?"

"Nah, let's get goin'."

An orderly wheels Levi to therapy. Soon he is following instructions, trying to lift one arm then another. The exercises were difficult, but Levi cowboyd' up. He was determined to get back to the ranch.

Later there was a knock at Doctor Blevins' door.

"Come in."

It was the orderly with a report on Levi.

"How'd he do?"

"Everything went quite well actually. He's trying very hard to get things right. If he progresses well, we should be able to send him home next week."

"He's always been a strong willed individual, I'm sure he'll work at it very hard. He wants out of here pretty bad."

After the orderly left, Sam picked up the phone. "Hello Kathy, is Jake around? Oh, I see. When he gets back will you please have him call me? I'd like to give him an update on Dad. Yes, he started it today and everything went well. He's trying very hard. Okay, just have Jake call me. Thanks, I'll talk to you soon."

Jake looked at Zeb. "It'll be good to get these geldings rode."

"Yeah, they're both comin' along real well After Javier puts about sixty days on 'em they should be ready to use."

"Yeah, I'm sure they will."

"Wonder how Dad did this morning? He was supposed to start that physical therapy today."

"If I know him at all, and I think I do, he'll be chompin' at the bit to get through it. He knows the sooner he improves the sooner he'll be gettin' home."

Jake nodded. "That' for sure! Pull in over by the barn. I think that's Javier and Carlos."

The pickup and trailer came to a stop.

"Buenos dias hombres."

"Buenos dias, Senior Yake. Hola Zeb"

"We have those two three year olds we were tellin' you about."

"Bueno. Carlos dame un mano."

The two vaqueros unloaded the two geldings and led them to the big corral.

"Donde esta es Senior Knight?"

"En la casa."

"Gracias, hombres."

"Por nada, Senior Yake."

The two men turned and started walking toward the house. On their way Mr. Knight saw them and walked out on the front porch.

"Howdy, boys, I see you brought those three year olds over."

"Yes Sir, we were hopin' Javier could put some time on 'em. They need some wet blankets."

"He's your man, for sure. Come in and have some coffee. What's the latest on Levi?"

"He was supposed to start physical therapy today. We left before we heard anything from Sam, but hopefully we'll get some news when we get back."

"I'm plannin' to go into town later. Think I'll drop in on 'im. Last time I was there he didn't know if he was punched or poured."

"Know what you mean. We've had days like that with 'im too."

"He'll be glad to see you for sure."

The conversation drifted from Levi to the drought and poor cattle prices while they finished off their hot C.

"Guess we'd better be gettin' back. Thanks for the coffee."

"Come back anytime, boys. It's always good to see you."

"Thanks Sir. Tell Dad howdy for us."

"Sure will. You boys take it easy."

Jake and Zeb walked back to their pickup and had a quiet ride home.

When they got there Kathy was waiting. "I'm sure glad you're back. Samuel called and wants you to call him."

"What did he say 'bout Dad?"

"He said he did well for the first day, but he wanted to talk to you."

Jake walked over to the phone and dialed the hospital. "Ma'am, this is Jake Blevins. Could I please speak to Doctor Blevins? Thank you; I'll hold. Sam! How's it goin'? Really? That's good to hear. Did he give 'em any uphill? I guess he knows he'd better do like they say if he wants to get home. Sure, we'll come in Friday about noon. Thanks Sam, we really appreciate the news. Adios."

"What did he say?"

"Well, he said Dad is takin' this real serious. The therapist went over what they had planned out for 'im and he really tried hard this mornin'. I guess the therapist feels he may be able to come home next week if he continues to work at it."

"That's wonderful! We have a lot to do to get things ready for him."

"Yeah, I need to build some sorta' ramp to get that wheelchair up, so we can get 'im in the house. I've got some material out in the shop. Zeb and me can get on it a little later."

"You didn't say how things went over at Mr. Knight's place."

"Went well...Javier likes the geldings, thinks they'll make some pretty good horses, 'specially the gray. Mr. Knight's goin' into town today—said he was gonna stop by and see Dad."

"I'm sure Pop will be glad to see him. They've been friends ever since I can remember."

"Hell Kathy, they've been friends ever since they were born. The Knight and Blevins families have lived around here forever. I know Old Man

Knight would do anything he could for Dad, and Dad would do likewise."

Kathy said, "Friendships like that are hard to come by in today's world."

"That's for damn sure. Hopefully his visit today will help get Dad motivated. I'm worried he's goin' to get discouraged. The injuries he's got are not goin' to be easy to overcome."

Kathy looked over at Jake. "We've got to encourage him all we can. When he gets back here to the ranch I'm sure his spirit will improve."

"I'm just concerned that if he doesn't improve he'll give up."

"I know, Honey. We just have to stay positive."

Jake walked over and put his arms around his understanding wife and held her tightly in his arms. "You'll never know how much I love and appreciate you!"

The front door slammed and they turned to see the kids walking in.

"Do you have anything to eat, Mom?"

"Put your books up and I'll see what I can find. How were things at school?"

"You know...same old stuff. We have some reviews coming up for finals. I'll sure be glad when we finish this semester. Have you heard anything about how Grandpa is doin'?"

"I spoke with Sam earlier," Jake said. "He said the physical therapy went well today. There's a possibility your grandpa can come home next week."

"Wow, that's great!"

"We have to get things ready around here for him. He'll be in a wheelchair, so getting around won't be easy for 'im. First thing we got to do is get a ramp built so we can get him into the house."

Kathy looked at them. "You kids can help a lot. We're all going to have to make some adjustments."

"You know we'll do anything we can to help. We want Granddad to get better as fast as he can."

"Well, then Andy, when your through with that pie, we'll go down to the shop and see what we have to build a ramp with."

Andy quickly finished off the pie and milk, and they headed to the shop. Zeb walked out of the tack room as they walked up. "What you two up to?"

"Talked with Sam awhile ago."

"How's Levi?"

"He said therapy went well today and that if he keeps it up he'll be able to come home next week."

"Damn that sounds good! It's a good thing I got his saddle put back together. He'll be needin' it."

"It won't be for awhile I'm afraid, but hopefully it won't be too long. Right now we have to figure out how to build a ramp so we can get 'im in the house."

"I'll give y'all a hand."
"We're countn' on your help for sure."

Chapter 15

Kathy looked out the screen door. "Boys you've done a great job on that ramp. We should be able to get Pop in without any problems."

"We sure hope so. Hopefully he'll understand it was necessary. He's so damn proud he won't want to admit that he needs it."

Zeb said. "Hopefully he won't need it too long. When do you think you'll bring 'im home?"

"Sam wants us to come in tomorrow. He called again yesterday and said Dad was progressing well."

Kathy came out onto the porch. "Come in the house. I've got some fresh coffee on and Sally baked a pie last night. She said she wanted to practice baking so she could bake for Pop when he got home."

Zeb grinned. "I'll come up and help him sample her baking."

Jake laughed. "You be sure to do that, Zeb. She'll put stock in your judgment for sure. Hell, I've seen you eat stuff that would gag a dog off a gut wagon."

"You two behave,"Kathy said. "Come in and have some pie and coffee!"

"Has Sam said what all he'll be able to do when he gets home?"

"Not really. 'Bout all he' said was that he's gonna have to keep up with his therapy out here and go into town once or twice a week for evaluation. The therapist wants us to watch him go through his therapy session so we'll know what to do out here. Sam did say he might be strong enough to use a walker in a little while."

Zeb shook his head. "You don't know how well you got it 'till you see somethin' like this."

"That's the God's truth, Zeb."

Zeb said. "I'm gonna ride out and check some of the tanks. We may have to start haulin' water if we don't get some rain pretty damn soon."

"That sounds good. I'm gonna' finish up a couple things around here."

Andy came into the kitchen. "Good morning, Andy. Your breakfast is about ready."

"Thanks, I'm pretty hungry this morning."

"We're going into the hospital in a little while. They want us to observe your Granddad while he's doing his therapy. We're supposed to be able to help him with it when he gets home.

Where's your sister? You need to leave for school pretty soon."

"You know her better than I do. She's always slow getting outta the bathroom in the morning. Seems to have a lot of war paint to put on."

Kathy walked into the hall. "Sally come on. It's getting late."

"Be right there, Mom."

A few minutes later Sally took her seat at the table. "Sorry I took so long. That smells good."

"Zeb and your Dad really liked that pie you baked."

"Did they? That makes me feel good. Hopefully Granddad will like me to bake for him when he gets home."

"After being in the hospital he'll like anything you bake, I'm sure."

Sally glanced toward her brother. "Well Andy, what do you plan to do for him?"

Before he could answer their mom interjected. "Your Granddad will appreciate whatever you two do for him, he loves you very much. You better get on the road or you'll be late for school."

They finished their breakfast and headed for the front door. "See you later, Mom!"

"Drive carefully, Andy!"

"Don't worry, Mom. I'm always careful."

"Looks like those two kids of ours got off to school a little late, didn't they?"

"You know how that daughter of yours is. She's always late getting ready."

"She's just a typical teenager. Wouldn't want her any other way, would we?"

"Honey, you're one of the most understanding men I believe I've ever know. Most men are very impatient when it comes to waiting on women to get ready."

"I'm just the picture of patience I guess. You 'bout ready to get to the hospital?"

"Almost... I will be pretty quick."

"Doggone it, you know we need to be there for Dad's therapy, we got to get goin'."

"What happened to Mr. Picture of Patience? Calm down, vaquero. We'll get there in plenty of time."

"Don't get your knickers in a knot, I'm just funnin'."

"You better be or I'll have to cut you off. You're getting a little too studly."

Jake pulled the car into the parking lot and circled around, trying to find an open spot. "Damn, this place always seems to be full. I'm sure glad we're takin' him home today."

They walked into the hospital and made their way to Samuel's office.

"Come in. How was the drive in this morning?"

Kathy walked over and gave Samuel a peck on the cheek. "It was delightful. Your brother was on pins and needles all the way in."

"Mornin' Sam, how's it goin'?"

"Everything is well. Dad is getting ready for his therapy. We better get you down there. The therapist wants you to get a good understanding of what she's doing for Dad. She feels it's very important that you both watch the various exercises so you can make sure he's doing them right."

Samuel took them to the therapy facility. "Janet, you know my brother and his wife, don't you?"

"Yes, we met briefly during Levi's occupational therapy. It's good to see you both again."

"Thank you Ma'am. We're glad to see you also."

"Please, just call me Janet. He'll be here shortly and we can get started."

An orderly wheeled Levi in. "Howdy Dad, you're lookin' good!"

Kathy walked over, leans down and hugged Levi. "It's sure good to see you, Pop."

"You two will never know how good it is to see you."

"Mr. Blevins, they're here to observe your therapy session. It's important they understand what we're doing so they can help you when you go home."

"You'll never know how good that sounds to me."

"We'd better get to it then."

An hour went by as Jake and Kathy went from station to station watching Levi perform various exercises.

"Some of the exercises will be done when you bring him in. We'll send print-outs of his exercises and equipment home with you."

"Hell, I could use those pulleys in the barn and wouldn't have to come to town at all."

Janet chuckled. "I'm sure you could Mr. Blevins, but we need to assist you here. We'll be increasing various exercises as you progress. When they remove your cast you'll be going to the therapy pool."

"We'll have him in here, for sure."

"Orderly, you can take Mr. Blevins back to his room and help him get ready to go home."

Levi looks up, holding back his emotions, "Thank you, Janet. I know I've been a jackass at times, but I truly appreciate all you've done for me."

"You just do what your supposed to at home and we'll get you back in the saddle. It's up to you now, Mr. Blevins."

The orderly took him back to his room while the others met in Samuel's office.

"I just want to go over a few things with you before you go. Dad is doing pretty well, considering. However, you need to keep in mind that the loss of tendon and muscle in his shoulder will prevent him from doing the things he used to do. The nerves won't regenerate and he might continue to suffer some paralysis. With continued therapy he may improve some, but we can't predict the final outcome. His age isn't in his favor. Even a young person would have difficulties. At his age it's going to be extremely difficult. Also, your going to have to be patient. He'll have some difficult days, and you know how his temper can get."

The room grew silent as Jake and Kathy struggled to understand the severity of the situation.

Jake finally said, "Well, guess we'd better get him home. He's probably chompin' at the bit to get outta here. Thanks Sam, and Thank you, Janet. We appreciate your efforts."

They walked to Levi's room where the orderly was assisting him with his belongings.

"Ready to go Pop?"

"Hell I was born ready. Let's get goin'!"

"I'll take that bag."

The orderly pushed Levi toward the exit as they followed closely behind. The doors opened and Levi was finally breathing fresh air.

Jake stopped and turned to his brother. "Samuel, I want to thank you for all you've done for Dad. We all appreciate it."

"You seem to forget he's my Dad too, little brother."

Jake grinned. "That's for damn sure, big brother. Don't be a stranger out there. Bring Verna and Randy out for dinner sometime."

"I'd like that, but with all the research and work here at the hospital, Verna and I don't see much of each other. She seems to have formed a new set of friends and they have a lot of activities they do together. Sometimes it takes up her entire weekend."

"Well bring Randy out anyhow. Dad loves that boy and would truly love seein' him."

"Sounds good to me, brother. I'll work on it."

Kathy brought the car up as the two brothers shook hands. Jake walked over to help the orderly put Levi in. He turned to Samuel. "See you later."

"See you later, Brother."

As they pulled into the driveway Sally ran out the front door. "Hey everybody, they're home!"

The car stopped in front of the house as they all ran to greet Levi.

"Hi Daddy. How's Granddad?"

"Take a look for yourself."

Sally ran around the car. "Hi Grandpa!"

"Well howdy there, princess."

"Andy, help me get this wheelchair out of the trunk."

"Sure, Dad."

Zeb walked up and leaned in as Kathy opened the door. "Howdy, you old reprobate. 'Bout time you got back to work!"

"That'll be enough outta you — you old codger."

Zeb proceeded to help Jake put Levi in the wheelchair and then pushed him toward the newly constructed plywood ramp.

"What in tarnation is this damn thing?"

"We built it to help get you into the house."

"Yeah Grandpa. We didn't want you tippin' over in the rocks!"

Zeb pushed him up the ramp. "We didn't want you causin' us anymore problems. Hell, you've taken enough time off."

They all followed excitedly as Zeb pushed him into the living room and stopped next to his favorite recliner.

"Give me a hand, Jake."

They picked Levi up to sit him in the recliner.

"Never thought I'd have to tote you like this. You're heavier'n half a beef."

"You won't have to long, you old moss horn. I'm gonna be on my feet sooner'n you think."

"I hope so. I'm tired of holdin' up your end of the stick."

"That's enough out of you two! Sally and I'll get some dinner on while you get the chores done. Pop needs some rest after that drive home. I'll bet you'd like some tacos."

"That sounds plumb larapin,' little lady. I haven't had anything like that since I went to the horsepistol!"

"Come on Zeb," Jake said. "Let's get the chores done. I could use some of them tacos myself." They headed out the door as Kathy and Sally walked into the kitchen.

Levi relaxed in his recliner. "Sure good to be home."

Chapter 16

Levi was in the front room doing arm curls with a one pound dumbbell. The phone rang and Kathy walked out and picked it up. "Hello? Well good morning to you too Samuel! He's working on it right now. He was very motivated when he saw Jake head out this morning. Yes, he was. Honestly, I believe if he could have gotten out of his chair he would've tried to go with him. That would be wonderful! Will Verna be coming with you? Oh... that's too bad, having Randy and you here will be a delight! Yes...I'll let everyone know. Okay Samuel, we'll see you on Sunday. Thanks for calling!"

Just as she hung up the phone Jake walked in the front door.

"Guess what?"

Jake studied her. "Can't imagine just tell me."

"Samuel just called. He and Randy are coming out to visit Sunday! Sally and I'll fix fried chicken for supper."

"Maybe that little talk we had at the hospital got to 'im. Is Verna comin' with him?"

"No, he said she had something else planned."

"Y'know. when we were talkin' the other day he mentioned she was spendin' a lot of time with friends. He seemed concerned bout it."

"That doesn't sound good, does it."

"No, it doesn't, but you know how those society people are, they always have to be involved in somethin'. Maybe she has some big charity goin' on or somethin'. Hell, who knows?"

"What's Samuel working on that takes so much of his time?"

"Don't really know. He never talks bout it. Must be some medical secret of some kind."

"Wonder what it could be."

"No tellin'. You'd think it was a nuclear bomb or somethin' the way he's so secretive. Whatever it is, it's playin' hell with his family life."

"I do hope they get things worked out. She's different from us, but she seems like a good person."

"I'll let Dad know they're comin' out. Maybe it'll perk 'im up a little."

Jake walked to the front room., and Levi looked up at him. "Have you heard how those geldings are doin'?"

"Not yet. They haven't been over there long enough. Soon as Javier puts some time on 'em I'm sure Mr. Knight will give us an update on 'em. Did he come by to see you last week?"

"He sure did. We had a hell of a good visit. Talked a lot 'bout the good old days when Fanny was still a girls name!"

"Samuel called."

"He did? What he have to say?"

"He and Randy are comin' out to see you Sunday. The gals are gonna fix fried chicken for dinner."

"Wonder what brought this on? Thought he didn't want anything to do with this outfit."

"Don't know, Dad. Maybe it was the conversation we had the other day when we picked you up."

"What the hell did you talk about?"

"Just family stuff. I think he's startin' to realize there is more to life than his research and work at the hospital. Hell, you never know 'bout him. He's a complicated man with some deep seated resentments."

"That's for damn sure. He never has forgiven me for what happened to Rita."

"Dad, it's just goin' to take more time. He'll come around."

Kathy came in. "What are you two up to? Can I get you some coffee?"

"Y'know little lady, I'd love some coffee."

"Sounds good to me too."

"Pop, Sally baked you a nice apple pie this morning before she left for school. Would you like some?"

"I thought I smelled somethin' bakin' earlier. It had my tape worm doin' back flips!"

"Think I'll join you two. I could use a little break before I start the laundry. Where's Zeb? Maybe he'd like to come in for some pie and coffee."

"He's been worried 'bout the water situation, an' rode out to check a couple of tanks. He's thinkin' we might have to start haulin' water."

Kathy left to get the pie and coffee.

"Jake you're a lucky man to have a wife like her. She reminds me so much of Rita."

"Believe me, I know that for sure. Don't know what I'd do without her."

It didn't take long for them to finish up the pie and coffee. "Boy that hit the spot. I'll have to make sure Sally's in my will for sure."

"Oh Pop, just let her know you liked her pie. She'll be happy."

Jake got up. "Think I'll put some more salt out and see if I can find Zeb."

"Yeah, and you'd better make sure we don't have any more of those cats around that nobody seemed to want to tell me about."

"We just didn't want to get you upset that's all."

"You handled it well. Gettin' D.C. out here as quickly as you did probably prevented more loss. He damn sure knows what he's doin'."

"He sure does. He had it figured out pretty quick when he saw the way that cat drug the calf off to feed her cubs."

"Whenever it gets dry like it is, they start movin' to where they can find prey and water. Sure hope we get a little moisture pretty soon!"

"Me too. I don't want to have to start haulin' water. Guess I'd better get goin'. See you later."

"Can I get you something else Pop?'

"No thanks. Think I'll work a little more on my arms and catch the news. Things are gettin' out of control in the world. It's got me worried."

"It sure has Jake upset. He can't believe what's going on in the Middle East. One of his old professors was working at the University of Beruit. I guess they had a lot of trouble there."

"It's troublesome for sure. I remember what we went through in Europe during World War Two. It's not easy to see people wounded or killed. Sometimes we have to make sacrifices that we really don't want to make."

"I know... Don't get me wrong. Jake is as patriotic as they get. He gets a lump in his throat every time he hears *'The Stars Spangle Banner.'* Guess he just can't let go of some things."

"We all have scars. Levi replied Some are just a little deeper than others"

Chapter 17

It had been a long, exhausting day as Doctor Blevins pulled off the hospital parking lot only to fight the miles of commuter traffic. Arriving home he walked into the entranceway of his spacious house over to a small table. He sat his briefcase down and began sorting through the mail. ."Anyone home?"

Verna walked into the room dressed in a nice party dress and putting on her earrings.

"Wow, where you off to?"

"I didn't know you were coming home this evening so I made plans to go out with some of the girls from the club. No big deal."

"You're dressed pretty fancy for it not being a big deal."

"Honestly Sam,— why should it matter to you? We never go anywhere together. You're always tied up at the hospital or in that thing you call a lab. I don't seem very high on your priority list."

"I'm just trying to keep your check book full."

"Well, keep up the good work, Red Ryder. I'll be back later."

She quickly walked out the front door, slamming it behind her. She got into her Mercedes and drove off.

Samuel walked to the door and watched her speedy departure, shook his head and walked back into the empty house.

Randy walked in, closing the door behind him. His dad was in the den reading a medical journal. "Howdy, Dad. You're home early. Where's Mom?"

"Oh she had something planned with her friends at the club. She left about an hour ago. Where've you been so late? Didn't you get out of school at four?"

"Don't you remember, Dad? I practice with the diving team after school."

"I'm sorry, Son. Guess I've been tied up so much at work it just slipped my mind. How's it going?"

"Pretty well, actually. I'm trying to perfect a difficult dive called the 203-C."

"I have no idea what that is. Can you describe it?"

"Well it's a back one-and-a half somersault, tuck. It's been hard for me to perfect off the three meter board. I really have to watch it or I might not clear the board!"

"Sounds pretty difficult to me. You be careful!"

"Ah don't worry. I'm gettin' the hang of it. Just a little more practice and I'll be good to go. I almost forgot—we have a practice meet in two weeks. Coach said we'll be putting in a lot of practice time between now and then."

"Don't wear yourself out too much. We're going out to the ranch Sunday to visit and have dinner."

"Great! It'll be good to see everyone again. I Can't wait to see Granddad. I'll take it easy tomorrow at practice."

"Are you hungry?"

"I'm famished. Swimming laps and diving really works up an appetite. I could eat a dead skunk!"

"Why do you talk like that? You sound more like your Granddad everyday!"

"I don't know Dad. After being at the ranch it just seems to come natural."

"I don't think I can find a place that serves road-kill, so how about a regular old steak?"

"Sounds like a winner to me!"

On the way to the restaurant, Randy looked at his father. "Dad, you seem like you're a thousand miles away. You haven't said two words since we left the house. What's goin' on?"

"I just have a great deal on my mind with work and all."

"It seems to me there's more goin' on than you're telling me."

"You're pretty intuitive, Son. I guess I should level with you and not treat you like a little kid.

You're probably not going to like what I'm about to tell you. As you're well aware, my work has been keeping me from spending a great deal of time with your mother and you."

"That just comes with the job doesn't it? I mean every doctor I know does the same thing."

"Yes, that's true for the most part... but I've become obsessed with my research, and if I'm not in the lab, I'm thinking about it every time I have a free moment. It's extremely important to me. My lack of spending quality time at home has created a great deal of animosity in your mother. You probably don't notice it like she does because you spend time at the ranch and school."

"Yeah, I stay pretty busy."

"Your mother doesn't have those things to keep her occupied. The bottom line is, I don't think she's going out with the girls from the club."

"What are you sayin'?"

"Randy, I...well, I think she's seeing another man."

Randy sat there motionless, trying to digest what he'd just heard. "Who do you think it is?"

"I don't know, but I'm going to confront her soon. I need to know.

The next morning, Randy headed out the front door headed for school and saw his mom coming up the walk. "You just gettin' home?"

Unsteady on her feet she walked toward the door. "Yes, we all had too much to drink last night so I stayed at Stella's. Where's your father?"

"He left about an hour ago. Said he had to make early rounds before he went to the laboratory."

"That's par for the course!"

She staggered through the front door and defiantly slammed it behind her. He turned to watch the spectacle, shook his head and headed to his pickup.

The day seemed to drag by as he tried to make sense of everything he'd been told and had witnessed.

"Are you okay, Randy?"

"Sure, Coach—just been thinkin' 'bout a few things."

"You better get your mind on diving. That 203-C dive you're working on can get you in trouble if you're not concentrating."

"No problem, Coach."

He swam a couple of laps, then headed to the three-meter board. Coach Willingham watched him as he prepared to make the difficult dive.

Randy sprang into the dive, his head barely missing the edge of the board. He came to the surface and swam to the edge of the pool.

"Son, I thought I told you to get your mind on your diving. You almost hit the board."

"I'm sorry, Coach."

"Get out and try it again. This time pay attention to what you're doing."

"Okay Coach, I'll get it this time."

He headed for the board and prepared to try it again. Concentrating, he sprang up again, this time nailing the difficult dive perfectly.

"That's more like it. Hit two more like that then swim four laps. That'll be enough for the day!"

"Okay Coach."

Randy took his time nailing two more dives perfectly, and swam his laps and headed toward the locker room.

"Come over here, Randy!"

"Yes Sir, Coach?"

"You're one of the best athletes we have in this school, but you're not totally in the game. You need to let go of what ever is bothering you. I don't want to see you get hurt. We have some practice meets coming up. They'll determine who goes on to state competition. I want you to be there, but if I see you struggling like you did today I'm going to bench you."

"Okay, Coach, I understand. I'll get it together."

Chapter 18

Andy looked down the dirt road for dust, the tell-tale sign that Randy and his dad were on their way.

In the house, Levi looked up at Zeb. "What time is it Zeb?"

Zeb pulled a gold pocket watch from his vest pocket. "'Bout eleven-twenty."

"Sure hope Samuel didn't change his mind. I'm sure lookin' forward to seein' Randy. Don't get me wrong, I'd like to see Sam too."

"We know, Levi. We can read the expression on your face clear as lookin' in a pool of artesian water. That Randy and you are so much alike it's scary."

Jake grinned. "You should know, you've known Dad longer than any of us. You two have been around the block once a ridin' and once a walkin'."

"Darn tootin' we have. Rodeo'd, fought the Germans, then came home and fought poor cattle prices and drought together."

Andy spotted a cloud of dust. "Here they come."

Levi grinned. "By God, they did make it Zeb."

Jake walked out to the car. "Howdy, Sam. Sure glad you two could make it. Everyone else is in the house with Dad."

Kathy opened the door. "Come in, come in. We're so glad to see you!"

Everyone walked into the front room.

Levi grinned "Well I'll be damned if it isn't Doctor Blevins!"

"How are you doing, Dad?"

"I've been better, but things are sure lookin' up. I've been doin' the exercises they sent home with me and movin' round best I can."

"That's good, Dad,. The better you stick with it the stronger you'll get. They'll be taking x-rays of your leg when you come in this week. Hopefully they'll be able to take that cast off."

Jake said, "That sounds good. Doesn't it Dad?"

"I'll believe it when they take it off."

Sam continued. "When they remove it, they'll get you started with a walker. You'll be able to get out of that wheelchair."

"I hope to hell you're right, Sam."

"Howdy, Granddad."

"Get over here you big booger! Give your old Granddad a hug!"

Randy leaned over and gave him a hug.

"I'm sure glad you made it out. I've been missin' you. What you been up to?"

"I've been goin' to school and workin' out with the dive team."

"How's all that goin'?"

"Pretty well, Granddad. I've been swimmin' a lot of laps and doin' some pretty difficult dives."

"It looks like it's agreein' with you. I don't think I've seen you in better shape."

"How are those two three year olds comin' along, Granddad?"

"They must be doin' well. Your Uncle Jake and Zeb took 'em over to Old Man Knight's place for Javier to ride for awhile."

"Hows that little gray doin'?"

"He ain't so little anymore. He's close to 15-1 hands and weighs close to a thousand pounds. Javier really took a shine to 'im."

"Wow, I sure hope I get to ride 'im."

"Don't you worry 'bout that; you'll get a lot of saddlin's on 'im."

Kathy said, "Come on, Sally. We better get to our cooking. You boys behave in here while we're gone."

Andy grinned. "Hey Randy how'd you like to look at the yearlings we brought in?"

"That would be great."

The boys headed for the barn as the others sat with Levi.

"Boy, that Randy sure is gettin' big. Pretty soon he'll be able to go bear huntin' with a kleenex and give the bear the kleenex."

Sam smiled. "He sure is. Sometimes I can't believe it's him. He's having a practice meet at the university pool next week. I know he'd sure like it if all of you could be there."

Jake looked at Levi. "What you think, Dad?"

"It would take a Blue Norther to keep me from it."

Zeb grinned. "I don't think there'll be any Blue Northers this time a year, Levi."

"Good, We'll tell him when he gets back."

Andy and Randy were looking over the top rail at the yearlings. "How do you think Granddads' doin', Andy?"

"It's hard to tell. He has good days, but then he seems to have to struggle to finish his exercises. He does 'em religiously, but he gets really discouraged when his hands and neck go numb. You can tell it really worries 'im. He gets very depressed."

"Do you think he'll snap out of the depression?"

Andy shook his head. "To be honest with you, I don't know. They say that nerve damage is why he experiences the numbness. The way I understand it, nerves don't heal up all that well. Remember the gray colt that ran into that pipe post during that lightnin' storm? That blow he took to his neck compressed some nerves. We tried hard to get 'im back to where he'd stand, but he got to where he couldn't even get up."

"I remember your Dad had to put 'im down."

"Well, I think Granddad thinks about that colt. I'm sure he wonders if he'll ever be able to stand and walk. He's worried he won't get better and it's causin' him a lot of depression. He's worried he won't be able to cowboy like he used to. It's taken the heart out of 'im."

Kathy walked out on the front porch and rang the triangle dinner bell. "You boys come and get it!"

"Wed better get to the house. Mom's got dinner ready."

"Thanks for bein' straight with me, Andy. I appreciate it."

The boys walked into the house.

"You boys get washed up and come to the table."

"Okay, Mom"

When everyone was at the table, Kathy said, "Jake, will you say grace?"

Levi interrupted. "Would it be okay if I offered the blessin'?"

She looked at Levi, surprised. "Why sure, Pop. You go right ahead."

"Lord, we are truly grateful to have this opportunity to be together. Thank you for gettin' Sam and Randy out here safe. We appreciate this fine dinner that Kathy and Sally Ann have fixed for us. Please let it nourish us and keep us strong. This we say in the name of Your Son, Jesus Christ. Amen."

Amens echoed around the table.

"Thank you, Pop that was a wonderful blessing."

Zeb smiled. "Didn't know you had it in you."

"What you think I am, some sort of non-believer or something?"

"Come on you two," Jake said. "Let's just enjoy the meal." He turned his attention to his nephew. "Say Randy, your Dad tells us you have a divin' meet comin' up next week."

"Yes sir, I sure do. It's a practice meet with a couple other schools in the area."

Kathy chimed in. "What Jakes wondering is whether you'd mind if the family came to watch you?"

"I'd love it if you were all there!"

Zeb said,"What 'bout me?"

Levi piped in. "Hell, Zeb I thought you already knew you're a part of this family. Hell, you've known me longer than anyone at this table."

"I truly appreciate that, Levi."

"Well, it's set then; you'll all be there."

"With bells on."

"Dad, I'll do all I can to get that cast off for you."

"That would be a true blessing."

Chapter 19

Standing near the pool with the dive team Randy saw his family walking in.

"Coach, would it be okay if I say hello to my family?"

"Sure, don't be too long. We have things to go over."

Randy trotted over to his family.

"Howdy, Granddad. I see you got your cast off."

"Yep, they took it off Tuesday. I'll tell you, it sure felt good to get it off. They showed me how to use this walker, and Kathy's had me on it every-day since. I'm gettin' along with it pretty good."

"That's great. How are all the rest of you doin'?"

Jake looked around. "Where's your Dad and Mom?"

"Dad called me from the hospital; they'll be here anytime."

Samuel walked through the gate. "Here's Dad now."

"Morning everyone, glad you could make it."

Levi looked up. "We wouldn't have missed it for the world."

"Where's Mom?"

"She had something to take care of, she isn't going to make it this time."

Disappointment and frustration crossed Randy's face. "Oh... I see." He tried to make excuses for her. "She probably has a charity event to attend. I'd better get back. Coach Willingham has some things to go over."

He turned and trotted back to where the coach was talking to the team.

Levi looked concerned. "Is he okay?"

"He gets that way before a meet," Sam said. "Guess he's got to get his game face on."

"Don't bullshit me, Son. That boy is stressed."

Samuel hesitated. "Looks like your getting along well with that walker, Dad. Maybe we'd better find a place to sit. Looks like they're getting ready to start."

The coach addressed his team. "Okay people I want you to swim a couple of laps, then get your warm-ups on."

As they started the laps he walked over to the family.

"Doctor Blevins, could I speak to you for a moment?"

"Sure, Coach Willingham." He looked at Levi. "I'll be right back. Don't go anywhere."

"Don't worry, Son. We're here for the duration."

When they put some distance between the family and themselves, the coach began. "Doctor Blevins, Randy hasn't been his normal self lately.

I'm very concerned about him. It's like he can't focus on what he's doing. His dives haven't been as strong as they have been in the past."

"We've had some family issues with his grandfather being injured. They're very close and I know he's been very concerned about him."

"I sure hope he snaps out of it. This dive he's doing is very difficult. Last week he almost hit the board. I don't want to see him get hurt."

"He should be okay once things get started."

"I sure hope your right."

"Thanks, Coach. I'll have a talk with him about it tonight."

The announcer began. "Testing...testing. Good morning, folks. We're about to get underway. Would you please clear the pool? Please clear the pool."

Randy and his teammates get out of the pool, put their warm-ups on and walked over to their coach.

"Okay people, stay focused on your dives. You've been doing well in practice. Now it's time to bring it home."

The announcer called over the chattering crowd. "Welcome, everyone, to the first practice meet of the year. We have some great athletes competing today. We hope you will enjoy today's diving competition. For those of you who are new to the sport, let me give you a brief explanation of competitive diving. The sport consists of performing acrobatics while jumping or falling into the water from a platform or spring-board. Scoring is based on the diver's approach to the dive, the flight of the diver and the entry into the water. Without further ado, let's get started. The school R.O.T.C. Honor Guard will post the colors. Please stand for the presentation of the colors and the playing of 'The National Anthem.'"

The last chords of *"The National Anthem"* drifted into the still air as the announcer called for the first competitor.

"Our first dive will be performed by Steve Sadler, a junior from Waco High. He will attempt a 101-A, a forward straight dive."

Steve approached the dive and sprang from the board.

"Well done, Steve," the announcer called. "That should score well. Our next competitor is Randy Blevins, a senior at Austin High. He will be doing a difficult 203-C for us. I understand he's been working hard to perfect this dive."

As he removed his warm-ups, Coach Willingham spoke quietly to him. "Keep your mind on the dive, Randy."

"No problem, Coach. I'll be right back."

Randy stood in the approach position, two to three feet back from the edge of the board, his arms to his side as if at attention. Trying hard to forget his personal turmoil, he walked to the end of the board and turned around to ready himself.

Springing up, he failed to get the lift he needed, and as he came over for the somersault his head hit the edge of the board, throwing him violently into the pool below. A stream of blood poured from his head and the water turned crimson.

Silence fell over the spectators as the announcer yelled, "Oh My God! Paramedics to the pool...paramedics to the pool...Oh my God!

Two lifeguards quickly jumped into the blood-stained water and quickly brought Randy to the edge of the pool as two others helped pull his limp body from the water.

Paramedics rushed toward the injured diver, carrying a backboard and rescue kits. Coach Willingham moved quickly to assist them.

The spectators watched the scene in horror, gasping as they gazed at Randy's motionless body lying at the edge of the pool.

Expressions of terror came over Levi as he gazed at his beloved grandson. "No...No Not Randy!" His head dropped as he fought back his emotions.

Doctor Blevins hurried to his son's side. "Support his neck and get that backboard under him, *now*!"

The paramedics gently straightened Randy's body, placing a neck collar around his neck and carefully slid the backboard under him. They put him on oxygen as they started an intravenous flow of Dextrose attempting to stabilize him.

"Randy...Randy, can you hear me Son?"

There was no response.

A gurney was brought in and they gently moved him onto it, Samuel assisted them as they pushed it to the ambulance.

Jake was at the back of the ambulance. "Sam, what do you want me to do?"

Getting into the ambulance he pitched Jake his car keys. "Find Verna and get her to the hospital, quick!"

"Where is she?"

"Hell, I don't know! Try the club."

The door closed and the defining sound of the siren blared as the ambulance headed toward the hospital.

Jake watched as it pulled away, then turned and walked over to his family.

Levi looked up at him. "How is he Jake?"

"I don't know, Dad... I just don't know."

Fear filled Andy's eyes. "Is he goin' to be all right?"

"I sure hope he is. Right now I have to find Verna and and get her to the hospital. Kathy, you take everyone back to the ranch. I'll use Sam's car to locate Verna."

There was fire in Levi's eyes. "There'll be no takin' me back to the ranch. Sam needs help right now and I'll be damned if I'm gonna sit around and wonder what's hapnin'. I'm goin' with you to find that damned socialite. Zeb, you take everyone to get somethin' to eat, then meet us at the hospital. We have to back Sam's play."

172

"No problema, Levi. Whatever you say."

In the car, Levi asked, "Do you have any idea where's she's at?"

"Samuel said to check the country club. If she's not there maybe somebody there will know where she is."

"This is a hell of a note. Randy's injured no tellin' how bad and she's off running around who knows where." Levi said with distain.

"Yep, not exactly your home-spun type of wife." Jake replied.

"Samuel deserves better than this. I never could understand why he'd marry a woman like that. All she cares about is his bank account. — Damn her black heart!"

"Dad, I guess it's not for us to say. Just some-thin' for us to watch."

"Yeah, but Sam's a damn good man and a good doctor. He needs a woman who'll appreciate him."

At the club, Jake and Levi slowly walked toward the entrance. "Wish I could move faster. This walker isn't the easiest thing to get used to."

"Just be careful. I don't want you fallin'. We've had all the problems we need today."

They slowly walked up to the desk clerk. "Excuse me, do you know if Mrs. Samuel Blevins is here?"

"May I ask whose asking?"

"Yes, I'm her brother in law and..."

Levi cut him off. "Yeah and I'm her father-in-law. Now, is she here or not, Sonny?"

"I...I'll page her, Sir. Paging Mrs. Samuel Blevins — Paging Mrs. Samuel Blevins. Will you please come to the reception desk? Paging Mrs. Samuel Blevins,—*please* come to the reception desk."

Shortly she arrived at the desk. "What are you two doing here?"

Jake started. "Well—"

Levi jumped in. "We're here to round up your sorry ass!"

"Really, Levi! You can't talk to me like that! I'll have you thrown out!"

Jake interceded. "Verna, there's been an accident. Randy was injured while diving at the meet."

Levi grumbled, "Yeah, an' they've taken him to the damn hospital!"

"Calm down Dad." Jake looked at Verna. "Sam asked us to find you and tell you to get to the hospital ASAP."

She looked at both men in disgust and ran out into the parking lot. The two cowboys walked to the entrance as she sped out of the parking lot, nearly hitting a golfer walking to his car.

"That hussy can drive!" Levi said.

"She sure as hell can. Here let me help you in." Jake helped Levi into the car and put the walker in the trunk.

"We'd better get down there pronto. Sam's gonna need our help for sure."

Chapter 20

Verna and Samuel were in his office having a heated discussion. "So what was so damn important that you couldn't be there to watch Randy? He's been so concerned about you he hasn't been able to concentrate on his diving. Coach Willingham told me he hasn't been doing well for a couple of weeks. He was afraid something like this would happen. I should have listened to him and pulled Randy out of the competition today. Now look what's happened!"

"Just a damn minute! You can't blame this on me!"

"The hell I can't! You running around like an alley cat in heat has had him upset for days! He's not a naive little kid. He sees right through you!"

There was a knock at the door. "Who is it?"

"It's me, Doctor. The emergency room nurse."

"I'll be right there."

He got up and walked to the door. "Do you have something for me?"

"Your son's CAT-scan and preliminary exams are completed. Dr. Fargo would like to speak with you and your wife in his office."

"Thank you. Please let him know we'll be right there."

They made their way to Dr. Fargo's office and knocked on the door.

"Come in... please have a seat."

Verna asked, "How is he Doctor?"

Doctor Fargo looked at them.—"Doctor Blevins, I know if my wife and I were sitting where the two of you are, you would be as candid as possible with us."

"By all means, Doctor. Please give us a truthful diagnosis."

Doctor Fargo paused as he peered into Verna's tear drenched eyes. "Your Son has suffered an open-skull fracture. There is evidence of intracranial hemorrhaging with evidence of cerebral edema and hemorrhage. He suffered a spinal cord burst and fracture of cervical vertebrae number two. We've placed him on a ventilator to maintain his oxygen supply. He's in a coma. We can only hope he comes out of it. If he does, he probably won't be the Randy you knew."

Verna sat there, her eyes transfixed as though she was a thousand miles away.

Knowing very well the severity of what they'd been told, Samuel finally spoke. "Wh— What do you suggest we do, Doctor?"

"My recommendation would be to maintain life support and observe him for forty-eight hours. God willing, we might see improvement. That will give you and your wife time to discuss things. I know you understand the gravity of the situation, Doctor, but you might need to help your wife understand it better."

Samuel stood and shook his hand. "Thank you for your candor, Doctor. We need to be with our family now." He took Verna by the arm to walk her out. She was sobbing heavily as they walked into the waiting room.

Levi looked up, anxiously. "Well how is he? What did the doctor tell you?"

"It doesn't look good Dad.— Verna and I want to thank all of you for your support today."

"You don't need to thank us, Son. We're your family. Can you give us an idea of how he's doin'?"

"Randy has suffered severe brain damage. His respiratory system is shutting down. They have him on a ventilator to maintain his breathing."

Kathy asked, "What can be done for him, Samuel?"

"Not much right now, Kathy. We just have to wait and pray it turns around for him. They'll observe him for forty-eight hours before they give us a prognosis."

Jake said, "What do we do in the meantime?"

Sam looked at his brother and in a low, soft tone said, "Pray like you've never prayed before, and then pray some more. Randy's in God's hands now."

Levi shook is head, then looked up. "Do you need any of us to stay in town and give you a hand?"

"No, Dad, but thank you for asking. We have a great deal to discuss and we need to be alone right now."

The spacious house seemed haunted as they sat in the living room having a cocktail. "Verna, I know I haven't been here a great deal of the time for the past two years. For that I would like to apologize. I've been totally obsessed with my research and the work I do at the hospital. I felt it was necessary for me to accomplish what I was working on."

"What was so damned important that you neglected your family?"

"It's not that easy for me to explain, but I'll do the best I can. Do you remember when I was doing my internship?"

"How could I forget? I was pregnant with Randy and big as a barn. You were at the hospital a lot then too."

"Yes... yes, as a matter of fact I was. Doctor Philips asked me to assist him with his research. I thought what he was doing may revolutionize medicine. He was researching adult and embryo stem cells. We transplanted healthy muscle and tendon tissue into injured monkeys and then injected stem cells. We were having a great deal of success."

"And you were assisting him with that?"

"As a matter of fact I was. He allowed me to work right alongside him, performing various experiments. I gained a wealth of knowledge from him. We studied embryo matter as well as adult bone marrow. Our work was progressing very well when he was killed in an automobile accident."

"Bet that put the brakes on your voodoo bullshit!"

"Actually, it didn't. I downloaded all of our research notes and brought them with me when I came here to work. That's what I've been doing in the hospital lab."

Verna got up, and walked over to the wet bar and poured herself a double shot of scotch.

"Okay, Doctor Frankenstein, why are you telling me all this crap now?"

"Because we're in this situation with Randy."

"You mean it will help our son?"

"Not exactly, but it could help Dad."

A bit tipsy she replied, "What's Randy's accident got to do with that old bastard?"

"Watch what you're saying. He's my Dad."

"Okay, what do Randy and Levi have to do with your witchcraft?"

"Verna, I don't think you really understood what Doctor Fargo was telling us today. As hard as it is for me to admit, he was telling us Randy is brain dead. He'll wait forty-eight hours, but in his gut he knows Randy isn't going to come out of it.

Verna jumped up, screaming and crying uncontrollably. "No... No, that isn't true! Randy can't die!" She threw her drink and the glass smashed against the wall.

"I'm afraid it's true. As much as it kills me inside, I'm afraid it's true!"

She stared defiantly at Samuel. "So what's it got to do with Levi?"

"You know Dad isn't recovering from his injuries very well. He has muscle and tendon damage as well as nerve damage. I'd like to extract bone marrow from Randy and Dad to see if there's a tissue match. If there is, I believe I can replace Dad's damaged muscle and tendon with Randy's. I'd use stem cells extracted and processed from Randy's hip to inject into Dad's hip bone. There's a chance it would improve Dad's recovery and possibly let him function as he did before his accident."

She glared at Samuel with hatred and contempt. "You damn fool! Do you know what you're saying? For God's sake you'll *kill* Randy! I've heard about all of this shit I want to hear! I'm going to bed!"

Samuel finished his drink, walked over and picked up a photograph of Randy.

He stared at it as he began to well up. "I love you, Son!"

Chapter 21

Verna walked into Samuel's office. "Good morning. Why didn't you wake me this morning before you left the house?"

"After last night I thought you probably needed the rest."

"Thank you for being so thoughtful, but I really wanted to come in with you this morning. Despite the fact that I was feeling a bit tipsy, I had a very restless night. I'd like to talk with Doctor Fargo. Is he in the hospital?"

"Yes, I saw him earlier when I was making rounds."

"Did he say anything about Randy?"

"Not really, he just said he'd like to talk to us later. Maybe we could get some time with him now."

"Did you see Randy?"

"Of course, I looked in on him earlier."

"How is he doing?"

"There's been no change in his condition. He doesn't seem to be responding to treatment. It would be best if Doctor Fargo explained his condition to you."

"Good morning Doctor Fargo. Do you have some spare time?"

"Of course...come in. Please sit down. I just made a fresh pot of coffee, would you like some?"

"No thank you, Doctor."

"I'm sorry I didn't have a lot of time this morning. It was just hectic in emergency."

"Not a problem. I have plenty of those days myself."

"They told me you were by to see your son this morning."

"Yes... Yes, I did stop by for awhile."

"Were you able to share your observations with your wife?"

Verna spoke up. "He tried, Doctor Fargo, but it would probably be better if you gave me your opinion."

He looked at her, trying to show compassion. "Mrs. Blevins, your son is not responding as we would like. His condition is extremely grave."

"What are you saying?"

"What I'm trying to help you understand is... what I'm saying is, there is little chance that he will improve."

Trembling, Verna looked at her husband and then Doctor Fargo. "What do you think we should do?"

"You and Doctor Blevins need to discuss what would be best for Randy. As I've tried to explain, it is unlikely he will regain consciousness.— If he does he will not be the person you knew as Randy Blevins. I know this must be painful for you to hear, but it's just the way it is. I wish I could give you a better prognosis but I'd only be misleading you. Maybe you should both go home now and talk things over. It can wait a little while."

Sam and Verna looked at each other knowing they must soon make a very difficult decision.

"Thank you, Doctor," Sam said. "I appreciate your professional courtesy."

"I'm sure you'd do the same for me."

Sobbing, Verna looked at Doctor Fargo. "Thank you Doctor."

He gave Verna a hug and patted Samuel on the shoulder as they left.

Randy's pickup was sitting in its usual spot when they pulled into the driveway. Verna looked at it tearfully.

"This just isn't possible! Surely there's something that can be done!"

Sam looked at her sadly. "All the discussion in the world isn't going to bring him out of the coma."

"I've been such a fool. If only I'd been there maybe this wouldn't have happened."

"Perhaps you're right. And if I'd have listened to his coach's concerns maybe I wouldn't have allowed him to participate. At this point we can't second guess ourselves. It's done." Sam sighed. "He's no longer going to be with us."

Verna poured herself a scotch and sat down.

"I've been thinking about everything Doctor Fargo told us and about your research. It all seems so foreign to me... like I'm stuck in a terrible nightmare." She paused. Before we go any further there's something else I need to tell you."

"What's that, Verna?"

"Over the past few months I've been seeing another man. I was lonely and needed companionship. You were so tied up with your work I felt totally left out."

"Do you really think I didn't suspect something? I was born in the morning, but it wasn't *this* morning. I'm not totally inept at seeing through things. Randy had his suspicions too. We discussed it just last week."

She sobbed uncontrollably, as though her heart is about to burst. "Oh my God... I've been so foolish! What do you want me to do? Do you want me to go back to New York?"

"We've all made mistakes. Mine was becoming too engrossed in my work and not spending more time with you and Randy."

He walked over and lifted her from her chair, then hugged her. "Your home is here with me. Remember, we married until death do us part. I love you, Verna."

She held him tightly. "I love you more than I ever realized. You're a strong man with a big heart."

"Maybe you should get some rest now. We can discuss it later."

"Thank you, Sam."

Samuel walked to the phone and dialed the ranch. "Hello. Yeah, Jake, I was wondering if you and Kathy would bring Dad into the hospital in the morning? Nine-thirty would be fine, and just come to my office. No, there's been no improvement that's what we'd like to talk to you about. Okay, we'll see you in the morning. Thanks, Jake."

He puts down the phone, walked over to the bar and poured himself two shots of bourbon. Deep in thought about his son, he walked to a window and stared at the empty pickup parked in the driveway. *If only Randy would get out and walk to the door.*

Turning, he saw Verna walk into the den. "I couldn't sleep. There's just too much on my mind."

She paused. "Sam...it's very hard for me to admit, but... we have to decide what's best for everyone concerned."

"I'm glad you've come to that realization. Have you thought about anything in particular?"

"First of all I've been thinking about what Dr. Fargo has told us. He's seen this before and what he said about Randy's future is no doubt the way things are. Also, I've thought about what you told me about your research. As hard as it is for me to say, I believe Randy would want to help his grandfather if he could, even if it meant him leaving all of us. They were so much alike, and he truly loved Levi. If you think your research will benefit your dad, then I feel we should proceed. There's no sense in prolonging Randy's suffering."

Sam nodded. "I knew you would eventually come to that conclusion. Guess I know you better than you thought. I spoke with Jake a while ago and asked if he and Kathy would bring Dad into the hospital in the morning. They'll be in my office by nine-thirty. I was hoping we could discuss this with them then."

"Sam you know this hasn't been easy for me to do."

"Believe me, Honey, it hasn't been easy for me either. I know what lies ahead to make this all work, and the process is difficult to say the least. I'll be working on my only son and my only father...and If I don't get it right we'll lose both of them."

"My God, Sam, I never thought of it like that!"

Chapter 22

"Honey I got a call form Sam a little while ago. Said he wanted me to bring you and Dad into his office in the morning."

"Did he say how Randy was?"

"Not really. All he said was it had somethin' to do with him. He sounded very peculiar."

"I wonder what on earth is going on. The last time we were there it seemed he and Verna weren't getting along all that well."

"That's an understatement. No telling what's goin' on with them!"

"It's really a shame. Basically she's a nice person."

"Yeah, but I think Sam's long hours and not bein' home really has gotten to her. I'm goin' down and let Zeb know we'll be goin' in early. I'd sorta like him to keep an eye on things while we're gone. When Dad wakes up from his nap you better let him know what's goin' on."

Zeb was at the round corral driving a two year old when Jake walked up. "How's it goin'?"

"Pretty good. This colt really pays attention. Makes it easier when they're like him."

"Listen, Sam called a little bit ago and wanted me to bring Dad and Kathy into his office in the morning."

"Did he say how Randy was doin'?"

"As a matter of fact he didn't. The conversation was pretty short. Didn't say much at all."

"Damn. Seems like he'd a let you know how he was doin'. He knows we're all worried sick over it."

"He didn't seem himself, like he was deep in thought bout somethin' and tryin' to tell me what he wanted all at the same time. Guess we'll find out in the mornin' what it's all about."

They arrived right on time, nine-thirty a.m.. Verna was talking with Samuel as they walked in.

Sam stood. "Come in. Good to see all of you. How are you getting along on that walker, Dad?"

"Ah, pretty good for a share-cropper."

Kathy said, "Morning, Verna. It's sure nice to see you again."

"Why thank you, Kathy. That's nice of you to say."

"Please sit down. Here Dad, I have this special chair just for you."

"That is a fancy damn thing. It'll make it easier to get back into my walker."

Sam looked at Jake. "How are things at the ranch?"

"Goin' pretty well. Zeb's been workin' with some of the colts. Haven't got any moisture yet. Hopefully we'll get some rain pretty soon."

Levi had heard enough. "Let's cut the crap. How's Randy doin', Sam?"

Samuel looked at his dad, trying to hold back his emotions.

"That's why we've asked you to come in this morning. We've been going through a living hell since the accident."

"We can only imagine," Kathy said. "We've all been worried sick."

"Thank you Kathy; we appreciate that. You all know I've been spending a great deal of time in the lab. I'm working on research that began when I was an intern at Johns Hopkins. I was working with a Doctor Philips on some very sensitive studies with tendon and muscle transplant. We were experimenting with adult stem cell therapy as it's applied to regeneration of tissue. Unfortunately Dr. Philips was killed in an automobile accident. I continued the research on my own. When I left to come here I downloaded all of our research material and brought it with me. I've been working on it here."

"So what's all that got to do with Randy?" Levi said.

"A great deal, but it also concerns you."

"What's it got to do with me, for Christ sake?"

"Give me a chance to explain, Dad. While working with Dr. Philips, we developed a means to use stem cells extracted from bone marrow to regenerate damaged tissue as well as improve transplanted muscle and tendon. He would replace damaged muscle and tendon with healthy tissue. He then administered stem cell therapy. We had very good success with the transplanted muscle and tendon tissue. The stem cell therapy helped the tissue to develop in the test animal to the point it was almost normal. The main concern we had to deal with was tissue compatibility."

Levi scowled. "Where are you goin' with all this, Sam?"

Sam looked over at his wife and tried to speak. "Well...see...Randy—"

Verna cut in. "What he's trying to say is that Randy is not going to recover."

Sam regained his composure. "Yes, that is correct, Randy is not going to come out of the coma. He's on life support and that's all that's keeping him going."

The others sat there speechless, looking at Samuel and Verna.

"We've talked this over at great lengths. What we would like to do now is let Randy help Dad."

"How in the hell can he help me if he's dying?"

Sam spoke quietly. "Dad... Randy can live on in you, if you'll agree to let me perform compatibility tests and transplants using stem cell injections."

"You mean you want to put Randy's tissue in me?"

"Yes. My research has advanced to the point that I can successfully perform these procedures in humans."

Jake said quietly, "Well, everyone always said Dad and Randy were like two peas in a pod. Maybe this will tell the story."

"I don't know about this," Levi said. "I don't want Randy's death to benefit my situation."

"Dad he's not with us anymore. Let him help you if he can."

Verna said, "Levi, I want you to know this wasn't an easy decision for us to make. However, under the circumstances it's the only right thing to do."

"Well, we're all family... maybe we should put it to a vote. You agree, Dad?"

"Guess so... if you all think it's the thing to do."

"All in favor of allowing me to proceed say Yes."

All but Levi gave their approval.

"Your vote, Dad?"

"I abstain, but will abide by y'all's decision."

"Fine, I'll arrange for the blood work and bone marrow test for tomorrow. Dad you'll have to stay in the hospital tonight so they can draw blood in the morning and prep you for an early bone marrow extraction."

"I thought I was through stayin' in this damn place."

"Not yet, Dad. We have quite a bit to do before you'll be out of here. But hopefully you'll improve quickly."

"Sam, could you give us an idea of how you're goin' to proceed and what we need to do to help, if anything."

"Sure, the first thing we'll do is draw blood from them and see if they are compatible. Then we'll extract bone marrow from their hip bones for a compatibility test. When we are satisfied they are compatible, we will proceed with the tissue transplants."

"How long is that goin' to take?"

"I'm going to put a rush order on it, so we should have the results by day after tomorrow if everything goes well."

Jake said. "Then what?"

"Then we'll proceed with the tendon and muscle transplants, using the healthy tissues from Randy. Once the tendon and muscle tissues are secured, we'll proceed with the stem cell injections, using the bone marrow host we've extracted from Randy's hip. It's immediately injected into Dad's hip ."

"What are the chances for all of this to work? I've never heard of anything like it."

"I feel strongly that they will be compatible. They've always had many similar physical characteristics, and they carry the same genes so they will be genetically similar. This is extremely important when doing Allogeneic Transplant."

"What happens when the stem cells are injected?"

"Simply stated, they begin to divide and eventually become mature blood cells. The red blood cells carry oxygen to all parts of the body. This in turn aids in cell and tissue repair."

"Do you really think this will work?"

"I've had success with this in the lab. I believe we have an excellent chance for success in this case."

Levi shook his head. "I always wondered what a guinea pig felt like. Now I know."

"Have I answered your questions well enough?"

Jake said, "Hell, I can't say for sure. I didn't understand a hell of a lot of what you said."

Kathy shook her head. "I don't know if anyone did. We'll just have to take Sam's word on it."

"We'd better get Dad checked in. They'll have to start getting him prepped for tomorrow's procedures."

"Would it be okay to see Randy before we leave?"

"Sure, Kathy. I'll take you to see him."

"Jake, after you visit Randy, please take Dad to Admittance. I'll write the orders and send them down."

"Sure, Sam, I'll get him down there."

Jake said, "Sam before I go I want to thank you and Verna for all your doin'. I know this can't be easy for you."

"Yes," Kathy said. "Thank you so much. Verna, thank you especially. I can't begin to imagine what you're going through. When this is all behind us, we'd appreciate it if you and Sam would visit us more often."

"We will. Having your support has meant a great deal to both of us."

Levi was holding back his emotions. "Verna, I never thought I'd say this to you, but from the bottom of my heart I appreciate all your doin'. That boy means the world to me. I just can't believe this has happened."

"Things sometimes happen for a reason, Levi. Maybe this was just meant to be."

Chapter 23

"How'd it go, Sam?"

"Very well," Jake. "We were able to get good cells from both of them. The specimens have been taken to the lab for compatibility testing along with the blood samples."

"How long before they determine the compatibility?"

"We should have the results back by mid-morning tomorrow. I've put them on a priority status."

Kathy said, "How are they doing?"

"There have been some complications. Randy's system didn't react well to the procedure." Sam paused a moment to fight back his emotions. "He is failing rather quickly. I want to proceed as soon as the test results are in."

"What do you want us to do?"

"I'd like both if you to stay in town tonight. Be back to the hospital by noon. The test results should be in by then. I'll schedule the procedures for two o'clock. If everything looks good I'll proceed. I'm going to be staying here at the hospital tonight to makes sure everything is ready."

"We'll pick Verna up on our way in."

"Thank you, I appreciate that. You're a very thoughtful lady."

"We're family, we have to stick together."

Jake looks up. "That's for damn sure, Honey."

"Dad's probably awake by now. Why don't you drop in and see him before you leave. I have some things to finish in my office."

"Fine, we'll see you in the mornin'."

"For sure, Jake. It's going to take everyone's prayers now. My associates and I will need all the help we can get."

Jake reached out and shook his hand and gave him a hug. We love you Brother."

They walked toward Levi's room as Samuel headed to his office to prepare for the next day's procedures.

The next day, Samuel was going over the test results as they walked in.

"Good morning. I'm glad you're all here. I've been going over the test results."

Jake said, "How's it look Sam?"

"Good. the blood and stem cell tissue are more than we could have hoped for."

"Does that mean you will be able to proceed?"

"Yes, Jake, the specimens show a very strong compatibility. You'd think they were taken from the same person. It's as good as it can get. I've never seen anything like it. They're both being prepared and we'll proceed shortly. I need to get ready now. I'll meet you in the waiting room as soon as we finish. You might want to stop by the chapel on your way. Like I said, I can use all the help I can get."

Trying to hold back her emotions, "Verna said, "Do you think I could see our son one more time?"

"We'd like to see him too if it would be okay."

Sam nodded. "You can't stay long; they'll be taking him to surgery soon. Come on; I'll take you to him."

Verna's eyes filled with tears as she looked down at her only son. "Oh my God... why Randy? Why couldn't it have been me?"

Samuel's emotions began to manifest themselves as he wiped his eyes and cleared his throat. "Jake, your going to have to take over here. I've got to stay focused on what I have to do."

"Don't worry, Brother. I'll keep things under control."

"Thanks." Samuel gave his brother a hug and turned to prepare for the task ahead.

A nurse approached them. "I'm sorry, folks. You'll have to leave now. We have to finish our preparations."

Verna leaned down and kissed her son for the last time. "I love you Randy."

Kathy put her arm around Verna, then leaned down and kissed Randy on the forehead. "We'll miss you Randy." She comforted Verna and assisted her out.

Jake stood there looking at Randy as they passed by, feeling as though his chest was about to explode. "You're a good man, Randy, and a damn good cowboy. I'll see you later."

Turning slowly he patted him on the arm and slowly walked out to join the ladies. "I think we need to visit the chapel. We have three men here who'll need God's blessings today."

As the little group waited, time seemed to drag. It'd been almost four hours since they left the chapel.

Jake looked at the women. "Could I get anything for you, Verna?"

"No thanks, Jake. I'm so numb nothing will help right now."

"How 'bout you, Honey?"

"No thank you, Jake. I'm fine."

Jake paced the floor, unable to sit for more than a few minutes. "I wonder if everything is goin' okay?"

"I'm sure it is. Someone would have informed us if there was a problem."

"Sure hope your right. I haven't had these feelin's since I ran point in 'Nam."

"Calm down, Honey. I'm sure everything is okay."

A nurse walked into the waiting room and approached Jake. "Mr. Blevins, the doctor asked me to let you know he'll be out to see you shortly."

"Thank you, Ma'am."

Shortly Samuel walked into the waiting room and over to the little group. "Everything went very well. Better than one might hope under the circumstances." He turned to Verna. "Honey, per our agreement his heart, lungs, liver, kidneys and corneas were harvested for transplant. He will live on in others as well as Dad."

Verna choked back the tears. "Thank You Sam. I know he would want to help as many people as possible."

Sam looked at the them. "We decided if Randy had to leave us, we would let him help others. That's why I was in surgery so long. Once I completed the procedures for Dad, I monitored the other specialists as they harvested the organs. I was there until they finished their work, then signed for his transport to the funeral home. Doctor Freedman signed the death certificate."

Jake squeezed his shoulder. "Sam, I know all this is hard on you. Can I ask? How's Dad?"

Sam nodded, the movement of his head almost erratic. "Everything went according to plan. He's in recovery and they are administering anti-rejection drugs and will continue to do so. I'll go over the next steps with you tomorrow. Right now I need to dictate my post-op. reports and file them. If you would, please take Verna home so she can get some rest. You and Kathy can stay at the house or drive in from the ranch. You should be able to visit with him in the afternoon."

Verna looked at him. "Sam, would you mind if I stayed with you? I'd feel better."

"Why sure, Honey. You can rest in my office while I finish my reports."

Jake said, "Okay Sam. We'll head out to the ranch. Everyone out there will want to know the score."

Kathy said, "You two take care now, if you need anything, call. We love you."

Verna forced a sad smile. "Thank you Kathy. I truly appreciate the support you have given me through all of this. It's more than a person could have hoped for."

Kathy hugged her. "Remember, you two need to come out more, especially when Pop gets home."

Jake and Kathy drove into the ranch as the others ran out to greet them. Andy ran up and before anyone could say anything he yelled, "How are Granddad and Randy?"

"Let's go in the house and your Mom and I will answer as many questions as we can. Have a seat, everyone, and try to relax."

"Can I get anyone something to drink?"

"No thanks, Mom. We just want to hear how they're doin'."

Jake slowly began to speak. "We all knew this wasn't goin' to be easy. In fact it's been down right tragic."

Zeb scowled. "Out with it Jake. What happened?"

"Settle down, Zeb. I'm doin' the best I can."

"To begin with, Dad and Randy had very compatible tissue and bone marrow, and—"

"Hell everyone knew that before they even took the samples. Those two have always been alike."

Kathy said, "Let him finish, Zeb."

Jake peered into their eyes, trying to muster up the words. "It's like this... Randy was in such bad shape they couldn't revive him. The life support system was all that was keepin' him alive. Sam and Verna reached an agreement that Sam should use Randy's muscle and tendon to improve Dad's condition. Unbeknownst to any of us, he's been workin' on these procedure for years. He felt his research had advanced well enough that he could perform the procedures on Dad. Now we just have to wait and see if it works out."

Andy looked at his dad, disbelief written all over his face. "Well, what about Randy?"

"Son... he didn't make it."

Sally looked at her father. "Oh No! You mean he's dead?" She ran to her mother, sobbing.

"Yes, sweetheart, Randy's gone."

A deafening silence surrounded them as they took in the devastating news.

Andy stared across the room, his eyes filling with tears. Zeb looked up at the ceiling, trying to hold back his emotions. "I think I'll walk down and check those colts. I need to get some fresh air."

Chapter 24

"Good morning."

"Good mornin', Andy. Did you get a good night's sleep?"

"Not really, Dad, I kept thinking about Randy all night."

"I know what your sayin'. Your Mom and I were just talkin' about it. It just didn't seem possible that this could have happened. It seems like it's just one thing and then another anymore. First Dad gets hurt and then Randy. God only knows what will happen next."

"What can I get for you this morning, Andy?"

"I'm not really hungry, Mom. I just wanted to sit and talk with you and Dad. Guess what I really want to know is if you'd let Sally and me go into see Granddad with you today?"

"What you think, Kathy? Shouldn't hurt for them to miss a day of school."

"Your Granddad would probably enjoy seeing the two of you. I think it would be fine."

"You better see if Zeb would like to go too. He's probably chompin' at the bit wonderin' how Levi's doin'."

"I'll go ask him... be right back."

The screen door slammed as Andy headed for the barn. "Hey Zeb, Dad was wonderin' if you'd like to ride in to see Granddad."

"I sure would. When are they leavin'?"

"In about an hour I guess."

"Tell 'em I'll be up soon as I get a few things done here."

"All-righty."

Out of breath from making the run, Andy walked into the kitchen. "Zeb said he'd be here soon as he finishes up with some things he's doin."

Rubbing her eyes, Sally walked into the kitchen. "Morning everyone."

"Good morning, Honey. You'll be going in with us to see your Granddad today, so have a little breakfast and get ready quickly as you can."

Again the car headed down the road, kicking up dust as it made its way into town for another trip to the hospital. The journey seemed to get longer every time they made it. Tensions were high with anticipation as Jake pulled into the hospital parking lot.

In the hospital, Jake said, "We'd better check in and see where he is." He approached the nurses station. "Excuse me, Ma'am. We're here to see Levi Blevins. Could you tell us what room he's in?"

She checked her computer. "He's in ICU, only family members are allowed to see him at this time."

Zeb stuck his chest out. "What you think we are?"

She looked up, startled.

"Sorry, Ma'am," Jake said. "Zeb here's just anxious to see his brother. I'm Doctor Blevin's brother and this is my wife and kids."

She looked them over. "Well okay... he's in ICU room 14. He's only to have three visitors at one time."

"Fine, Ma'am. Thank you."

Looking into room 14 they were surprised to see Verna sitting next to Levi. Jake and Kathy walked in as the others remained at the door.

"Hello, Verna," Jake said. "We didn't expect to see you here this early."

"I came in with Samuel. I wanted to be with Levi while he made his rounds."

"Has he come around any?"

"Yes, but he's very sedated. He thinks I'm Rita. I'll go get some coffee so all of you can visit with him. Samuel should be in his office soon."

"Thanks, Verna."

They sat there with him awhile and then let Zeb come in to see him. He looked at his old compadre lying there motionless. "You old fart, I hope to hell all of this gets you back to work. I'm tired of holdin' up your end of the stick."

Levi tried to focus. "Zeb? That you? Rita was here awhile ago. Did you see her?"

"Yeah...Sure, Levi. She's takin' a breather right now."

Hearing the jumbled conversation, Andy and Sally walked in.

"The kids are here too, Levi."

He tried to focus on his grandchildren. "Hey...ain't you... s'posed to...be in school?"

"We took the day off," Sally said. "Andy and I just had to see how you were doing."

"Yeah Granddad. We couldn't wait any longer."

"Well...sure glad... y'came in." He drifted back to sleep.

Their dad walked in. "Kids, we better leave him be. He needs a lot of rest."

"Yeah, the old geezer has had his hands full. He needs a siesta."

"Kathy, why don't all of you visit with Verna in the cafeteria? I need to check in with Sam."

There's a knock at his door. "Yes, who is it?"

Looking in as he opened the door. "It's me Sam."

"Well, come on in."

"How are you today, Sam?"

"Pretty good, just tired. Have you been to see Dad?"

"Yeah, we brought Zeb and the kids in to see 'im too."

"I saw him earlier when I was making my rounds. He was pretty sedated, not saying a whole lot. Kind of a change for him."

"Isn't that the truth. He wasn't sayin' much when we saw him either."

"We just need to keep him quiet for a couple of days; then we can start getting him up and around a little."

Jake looked at his brother and hesitated. "Sam, I hate to bring this up, but... what are your plans for Randy's services?"

"Thanks for asking. We've been talking about it quite a bit. We'd like to wait until Dad is released from the hospital. We're sure he'd want to be there."

"When do you think that will be?"

"If all goes well he should be out in a week. In the meantime we'll publish Randy's obituary and let people know funeral arrangements are pending. I'm sure his coach and teammates will want to attend."

"I'm sure there are a lot of folks that will want to be there. What can we do to help with the arrangements?"

Samuel looked at his brother trying hard to hold back his emotions. "Well, Verna and I were hoping it would be agreeable with all of you if we buried him next to Mom at the ranch."

"Sam that would really make Dad happy knowing he was there with her."

"Would you mind getting it prepared? Just a simple graveside service is what we were thinking."

"Consider it done.."

"Thanks, Brother. I knew you'd be there."

"Never doubt that, Sam... Well, guess I'd better get everyone home. We have chores waitin' for us. Give Dad our best when he comes around. He probably won't even remember we were here."

"He probably won't, but I'll make sure he knows you were."

"Thanks, Sam."

"See you later, Jake."

Chapter 25

Two days later, Samuel walked into ICU 14. "How are you today, Dad?"

"My head seems a little clearer today. You heard anything from Jake? Seems like he'd let me know how things are goin' at the ranch."

"They all were here to see you day before yesterday. You were still pretty well sedated and just don't remember them being here."

"Did Zeb come in?"

"Yes, he was here also. You seemed to respond to him more than any of them."

Levi shook his head. "Wow, this medicine can really play tricks on a fella."

"I'm going to examine your shoulder this morning. I want to make sure everything looks okay."

Samuel removed the dressing and looked at the incision.

"What you think, Son? Am I gonna make it?"

"This is unbelievable. The incision looks like you've been post operative for a week. This isn't natural."

"What do you mean?"

"What I'm saying is your healing at an unbelievable rate. I'm going to have Doctor Franklin examine you. He's the surgeon that assisted me during the procedure."

Samuel picked up the room phone and called the nurses' station. Have Dr. Franklin come to ICU 14, please. Thank you."

"Paging Dr. Franklin... Paging Dr. Franklin... please go to ICU 14."

"Dr. Franklin walked in a few minutes later. "Good morning, Doctor Blevins. How's our patient coming along?"

"Better than I expected. I'd like you to give me your opinion of the incision."

Dr. Franklin walked over to Levi and lifted the gauze bandage and began examining Levi's shoulder. He looked up at Dr. Blevins in amazement. "Doctor Blevins could I speak to you privately?"

"Sure."

Levi looked worried. "What the hell is goin' on Sam?"

"Don't worry, Dad, we just need to discuss a couple of things. We'll be right back."

They walked out into the hallway and Doctor Franklin looked at Samuel. "That's the most incredible thing I've ever seen. His incision looks like it's at least a week post-op."

"I know. I couldn't believe it either. That's why I called you."

"Do you have an explanation for it?"

"The only thing I can think of is their bone marrow and tissue match. They were the most exact I've ever seen."

"Yes, I'd never seen anything like that either. Do you think his accelerated healing is a result of that?"

"What else could it have been? Most surgery takes weeks to progress to this point. If his recovery continues at his rate he'll have normal use of his shoulder within a month or two. Hopefully the nerve damage will respond as quickly."

Doctor Franklin smiled. "Not only that–if he continues to recover like this it's going to be very controversial in the medical community for quite some time."

"Without doubt the research that Doctor Philips started with stem cell treatment when applied to tendon and muscle transplant will prove to have merit."

"Well, he started it, but you have developed it to the point that it gave validity to the procedure. The work you've done in this case is far beyond anyone's expectations. There is now solid evidence of the merits of stem cell therapy."

They looked at each other and turned to walk back into Levi's room.

"Okay, Sawbones, what the hell is goin' on?"

"I'll let Dr. Franklin explain it to you."

"Well Sir, it seems you're recovering at a much faster pace than is normal even for routine surgeries. The surgery you had was far more complicated than normal shoulder surgeries. Doctor Blevins has accomplished something that has previously only been medical theory."

"Enough beatin' around the bush. Get down to the nut cuttin'."

"Mr. Blevins, your Grandson Randy and you were so genetically matched that when you received muscle, tendon and bone marrow tissue it accelerated the healing process in your body."

The doctors looked at each other and then at Levi.

"Dad, your accident at the ranch and Randy's accident might have been the catalyst that will help thousands of people who have had problems similar to those you've experienced."

Levi looked down and shook his head, then looked back at the doctors. "I just wish it could've been the other way round for Randy and me. I've had a good life an' he was just gettin' started."

"I know, Dad, but this is the way it is. We have to see where it takes us."

Dr. Franklin said, "I think we better let your dad rest now."

"Good idea, and we need to record our observations. I'll be back later Dad."

Samuel had turned to leave when Levi slowly spoke. "Sam, when are Randy's services to be held?"

"We were waiting to see how you progressed. We knew you'd want to be there."

"What are your plans now?"

"Jake is helping us with the arrangements. We all thought it would be appropriate to have him placed next to Mom at the ranch."

A grateful but surprised look came over Levi's face. "That's the best thing I've heard since this nightmare started."

Levi turned his head just before a tear rolled down his weathered face.

Chapter 26

"Who were you talking to?"

"It was Sam. He was givin' me some information on Dad."

"Is he all right?"

"Accordin' to Sam he's better than all right. It's hard to believe actually."

"What did he say?"

"Well it seems the procedures they did on Dad are healin' rapidly. They are quite advanced considerin' he was operated on just a few days ago. Sam said that he and Dr. Franklin both examined him yesterday and the shoulder looked like it was at least a week post operative. They couldn't believe what they saw. He said the therapist is going to start him in one of those walkers today. They might even put him through some light shoulder exercises to see if the tissues they transplanted are as far advanced as the incision."

"My gosh. How can that be?"

"He thinks it's related to the fact that Dad and Randy had such strong genetic compatibility. He's goin' to let us know how the therapy session goes."

Doctor Blevins walked into the therapy center. "How did he do today?"

"I was quite surprised actually. We put him through a light workout with the walker and he did exceptionally well, so we put him in the therapy pool for about fifteen minutes. The staff was quite impressed with him."

"How do you think we should proceed?"

"If he continues like this for the next two days I think we could release him as an outpatient. It will be important for him to continue with the exercises we send home with him, and he should come back twice a week so we can work with him in the therapy pool and observe his progress."

"Thank you, Janet. Please let me know how he does over the next two days."

"I certainly will, Doctor."

"Think I'll check in on him. Talk to you later."

He walked into Levi's room. "Hello there, Senior Blevins. How are you feeling after your work out?"

"Fit as a fiddle. Enjoyed gettin' in that big tank."

"The therapist said you did well today. They were all impressed with your progress."

"Good, then when do I go home?"

"If you keep up the good work it might be in just a couple of days."

"That's the best news I've heard all day. This place is depressin'."

"You just be a good patient and do as they tell you and you'll be out of here before you know it!"

"Thank God."

"I'll be back in a while. I have some other folks to check in on. See you later."

As he walked out he heard a page. "Doctor Blevins, you have a phone call on line two."

He walked to the nurses' station and picked up the phone. "Yes? Oh, hello Honey. How are you? Good. He's doing very well; they had him in therapy today. Maybe in a couple of days. Yes, I was thinking about that myself. I'll call Jake and ask him to proceed with everything. Yes, I'll let you know. You rest now. I'll be home by six. I love you too...'bye now."

He hung up the phone and finished his rounds, then went into his office to phone his brother. to ask him to make the final arrangements for Randy's funeral.

Two days of therapy passed quickly, and Jake and Kathy were at the hospital to pick up Levi.

Samuel explained Levi's progress to them. "He's been doing quite remarkably actually. The staff has a difficult time believing how well he's done."

Jake asked. "When will he be ready to leave?"

"We'll have to meet with him and the therapist and go over his therapy routine; then he should be ready to go."

"Sam you don't know how much we respect what you've accomplished. The work you're doin' certainly will help a lot of people in the future."

"Let's hope so, Brother. We need to meet with Dad and Janet. She can fill you in on what needs to be done."

They walked into the therapy center and Levi was sitting at Janet's desk. "Come in, folks. It's good to see you again. We were just going over a few things here. Doctor Blevins, thank you for joining us. I just gave your dad copies of the exercises he has to do at home. Nothing complicated, and he has all the supplies he'll need from his previous therapy. What's important is for you to bring him in on Tuesday and Thursday. We'll work with him in the therapy pool as well as his normal routine. That way we can document his progress. Do you have any questions?"

"I told her I could use that metal stock tank at the ranch and I wouldn't have to come to town at all."

Kathy smiled. "There's a little more to it than that, Pop. Janet, is there any special diet I need to prepare?"

"No, not really. He'll be continuing his medication so make sure he has something on his stomach when he takes it. Other than that he can eat about whatever he wants. Are there any other questions?" She paused. "Okay, then I guess I'll turn him over to all of you."

Jake holds out his hand. "Thank you for all you've done. Our family truly appreciates it."

"It was my pleasure, Mr. Blevins."

"Jake... just Jake." He glanced toward his dad. "That's Mr. Blevins over there."

They began to file out, Levi moving cautiously with the walker.

Jake said, "Folks you go on ahead. I'd like to talk with Sam for a minute."

As Jake and Sam stopped, Kathy continued to walk next to Levi as they made their way to the exit.

"Sam," Jake said. "I went ahead and finalized things for Randy. Hope you don't mind. I set the services for next Saturday at ten in the morning. That should give folks plenty of time to get out there. Some of our neighbor ladies and folks from church are bringin' food for everyone. I spoke with Coach Willingham and he's arrangin' for a bus to bring out the team and others from school. The choir will be doin' the singing."

Tears welled up in Samuel's eyes as he hugged Jake. "From the bottom of my heart I thank you, Brother."

As Jake caught up with Levi and the others, Kathy asked Levi, "Can we stop and pick anything up for you, Pop?"

"No thanks. I just want to get back to the ranch. There's nothin' I need in here."

"Okay we'll just head to the house."

Levi looked up. "Jake, has there been any arrangements for Randy?"

"Yes, Dad. Everything is set for next Saturday. We were waitin' to see when you'd be able to attend."

"Thank you, Son. That boy meant the world to me. For the life of me I can't believe all of this has happened. It seems like everything is spinnin' out of control."

Saturday arrived and people were congregating at the graveside.

Levi had a stern but sorrowful expression as he sat there staring at the casket. Sitting next to him, Verna sobbed as she wiped her eyes. There wasn't a dry eye in the congregation.

The pastor walked to the end of the casket and begins to speak. "We're here today to pay our respects to a fine young man who was loved by each and every one of us. He loved it out here on this ranch, so it's only befitting that he rest here now. Randy always did his best with school, athletics and being a good cowboy. He loved his family, and his friends always knew they could count on him if they needed a hand. He was just that kind of young man. He's with us now and will forever be in out memories."

As he concluded his remarks the choir stood and sang *"Amazing Grace"* then returned to their seats. The pastor stood to give the final prayer.

"Our Father in heaven, we thank you for giving us the opportunity to know this fine young man.

We ask you to bring him into your Heavenly Home. Watch over his family and grant them peace in their hearts— Amen."

"Amen" rang throughout the congregation.

Kathy said, "On behalf of the family I'd like to thank all of you for being here. Many of you brought food, which will be served at the house."

Verna smiled. "Thank you, Kathy. You're a jewel."

"I know you would do the same for us. Just remember you and Sam need to come out more."

"Believe me, we certainly will."

Zeb and Andy helped Levi to the pickup as the others returned to their vehicles.

Levi said, "Take me down to the barn. I need to talk with you and Andy."

As they pulled toward the barn, Jake and Samuel were helping their wives out of the car. "What's up with them?"

"Hell if I know, Sam. Let's get the ladies in the house and see what's goin' on."

"Yeah, I think we better."

Neighbor ladies from surrounding ranches began to serve everyone as Jake and Samuel excused themselves and headed toward the barn.

Levi said, "I wanted to talk to you two before I discussed my plans with Jake and Sam."

"What about, Granddad?"

Just as he was about to answer his two sons walked up. "What you three got goin' on down here? You got a jug hid out or somethin'?"

"Yeah, and there's just enough for the three of us. You get your own damn jug."

Zeb and Andy remained silent.

Levi grasped the walker that seemed to be holding him upright.

Zeb finally spoke. "Why are we down here, Levi?"

Levi looked at the four men staring back at him with puzzled expressions. "Well, fellas, it's like this. The wreck I've been in for the last couple of months has put a terrible strain on finances around here."

"Yeah Dad, but we're managin'. Besides, what's that got to do with bein' down here?"

Levi shook his head. "I don't know rightly how to tell y'all 'bout what's goin' on with me."

Samuel looked up. "What do you mean? What's going on Dad?"

"Well ever since you operated on me I've had some strange things goin' on with my body."

"Like what?"

"Here... let me show you."

Levi set the walker aside and began to walk around, easily raising his arms. They watched him, amazed at what they were witnessing.

"My gosh, Granddad!"

"I can't explain it. I haven't felt this strong since before my wreck."

"You're responding far beyond my expectations. This is unbelievable!"

Jake looked at his brother. "What the hell is goin' on, Sam?"

"I believe the stem cells were such a strong match that the transplant and damaged tissue is responding at an unbelievable rate. It's far more advanced than anything I've ever seen or heard of."

Levi nodded. "This is what I wanted to show Andy and Zeb. As I was sayin' before, I feel responsible that our finances are flatter than piss on a plate."

"Dad we just want you to get better. Quit worryn' 'bout money."

"I can't stop worryn' about it, and I've got a plan to help the situation."

"What sort of plan?"

"I'm goin' to start my own physical therapy program. I'm gonna have Zeb build me a ropin' dummy and I'm gonna' start practicin' with a rope. I used to be a fair calf roper."

"Dad, I don't think your ready for that." Sam said. "Besides, they call it tie-down ropin' now."

Levi glared at him. "The hell I'm not. If I keep improvin' like I am I'll be ready to go down the road in a month or so."

"Come on, Dad, you know better than that. These youngsters today are a bunch of wolves."

"We'll see about that."

Zeb looked at his old friend. "If you want me to build you a ropin' dummy, Levi, consider it a done deal. Nobody ever could change your mind once it was set on something."

"Okay Dad, if you think you can handle it I see no reason to try and stop you. However, I want you to still come in for at least one weekly check up."

Jake said, "Sam, do you think this is smart?"

"I wasn't expecting this type of recovery. If he thinks he can handle it, let's let him. Nothing else has been normal with this case. We might as well see where it goes."

Jake looked at the ground and shook his head. "If you say so. You're the Doc. We'd better get up to the house and visit a little with our guests before they leave. Whose gonna tell the others 'bout this?"

Zeb put the walker in the pickup as Levi got in. The others watch and then walked toward the house.

A few hours later, Sam said, "Sure was good to see so many familiar faces again."

"Maybe you should hang around out here a little more. There's some fine folks in these parts."

"I hadn't carried on a conversation with Old Man Knight in quite some time. Sure was nice that he brought Javier and Carlos. They're sure good men."

"Yeah and damn good cowboys."

As the last car pulled away they waved and went into the house.

"Anyone for some coffee?"

"Sounds good, Honey."

Verna said, "Here let me help you."

Kathy smiled. "Thanks I appreciate the help. You need to learn your way around here anyhow since you and Samuel will be visiting more often."

Sally followed them into the kitchen.

"Okay whose gonna tell 'em 'bout Dad's plan to start ropin' therapy?" Jake asked.

They all looked at each other with a bit of fear on their faces, knowing the shit would hit the fan when the ladies heard the news.

Sam said, "Maybe I'd better."

Zeb piped in. "Yeah maybe you better seein's how you're the one that created this monster, Doctor Frankenstein."

They all laughed except Levi, who didn't even crack a smile. "Go ahead and laugh. You'll soon see I'm serious as a hen layin' about this."

The ladies returned with coffee and cookies and served each of them.

"Ladies, you better sit down. Sam has somethin' to tell you."

When the ladies settled, Sam began. "Well as you know, Dad has had a rather unusual rate of recovery since the surgery."

"Yes, but this has been good hasn't it?"

Sam nodded. "Yes, it is. It's so good that he feels he wants to start his own physical therapy routine."

"What are you saying?"

"What I'm saying is the muscle, tendon and nerves in his shoulder and arm have improved to the point he feels he can swing a rope."

"What? Are you telling us that Pop's improved to the point he can actually do that?"

Levi looked at the ladies. "That's exactly what he's telling you. I feel stronger than I did before my wreck. In fact, I feel better than I have in years. I'm gonna' start practicin' on a ropin' dummy. Then, when I feel up to it, I'm goin' to the practice pen on horseback."

The ladies looked at each other, not believing what they'd just heard.

Verna's hand went to her mouth. "You can't be serious, Levi!"

Zeb said, "He's as serious as a heart attack after an eight dollar cheeseburger."

Levi looked around the room at each of them. "I have to do this for all of you, but for two people in particular: Randy and Samuel. I can't let what they did for me go without some sort of payback. Besides, maybe I can pick up a little dinero to pitch in the hat for expenses around here."

"Do you really think you can do this, Pop?"

He looked at her with determination in his eyes. "Yes, Kathy I believe I can."

Chapter 27

"Holy cow, Zeb! This is tougher'n I thought it'd be."

"You knew it wasn't gonna be easy. It's been years since you roped competitively."

"I know, but I'm feelin' stronger everyday."

"You're doin' pretty damn good considering all you been through."

"It's like I was twenty years old again."

He threw one loop after another, not wanting to let up, and he got more accurate with each throw.

"I've got a little competition goin' with myself. I have to make twenty-five good catches in a row. If I miss I have to start over."

Zeb watched his old buddy counting each good loop.

"Hell, Levi, I think that last one was twenty-five in a row."

"Yeah I think it was. I'm gonna' quit for the day, I have to go into town tomorrow for a check up. I don't want to be too sore."

"Mr. Blevins, I'm going to ask you to do a few movements with each arm. Dr. Blevins will take notes on your ability to perform the movements."

"Dad, once we've completed these tests we want to get another MRI."

"Are you goin' to ear mark and brand me too?"

"No, Dad, but we might go ahead and castrate you."

Levi looked at his Son. "That'll be the day."

With the MRI completed the doctors were going over the other test results with him.

"Mr. Blevins, whatever you're doing for your physical therapy, keep it up. Your recovery is astounding. Not only have we not seen anything like it. We've never *heard* of anything like it. Dr. Blevins has made major breakthroughs with his research. Now, his surgical techniques will be studied by doctors around the world. This may end the controversy over the merits of stem cell therapy."

"You see, Dad, your body has accepted the new muscle and tendon. There is no sign of rejection. The stem cell therapy has aided other muscles in your body to regenerate as well. You have the muscle tone of a much younger man."

Levi looked at the two doctors, trying to hold his composure. "Yeah, thanks to Randy."

"Yes, and thanks to Doctor Blevins for his dedicated research and outstanding surgical skills."

"Dad, we'll have the MRI results back in a couple of days. We'd like to see you back here next Wednesday."

"Sounds good to me. I'll get Jake to bring me back in."

"Remember, Mr. Blevins, whatever your doing for physical therapy keep it up, it's working."

Jake walked up as they left the office. "Afternoon. How'd it go?"

"It's all looking very positive, Jake. Your Dad can fill you in. I don't mean to run off like this but I have a couple of patients to check on. Please excuse me."

"Dad's coming along well." Sam said. "His body is accepting the muscle and tendon and his range of motion is better than we expected."

"That's great news. I can't wait to get home and tell everyone."

"I hate to have to leave you, but I have some patients to see as well."

Levi nodded. "No problem, Son. See you next week."

The three of them shook hands and Levi gave his boy a hug. "Thanks, Son."

Zeb watched him practice. "Hell, Levi, you're lookin' pretty damn good there."

"It's comin' along. Think I'll be ready for the practice pen pretty soon."

"You think so?"

"Yep." He coiled his rope and hung it on the dummy. "How'd you like to take a little ride?"

"You mean a horseback?"

"Of course a horseback, you blamed fool."

"Don't get your shorts in a twist. I'll saddle some horses."

A short time later, Zeb led a nice Buckskin over to Levi and handed him the reins. "Here you go."

Concerned about him, he watched Levi struggle a little to get mounted. "Can I give you a hand?"

"Hell no! I need to do it myself." He finally settled into the saddle. "Whew! I made it."

"Yep. Now let's see if you can stay there."

Levi rode into the round corral and walked his horse in a circle, kicked him into a trot and then a lope—then cut an eleven as he reined him in. "Let's take a little ride, Zeb."

"Let's do it." Without dismounting he opened the gate, allowing Levi to ride through.

"So far so good."

The two old cowboys rode into the open pasture.

"Damn, I sure needed this. I'm stiff as a board."

"You look like you're a doin' pretty damn good to me."

They rode for about half an hour then headed back to the barn to unsaddle.

"Where you two been? I've been lookin' all over for you."

"Levi here wanted to make sure I did a good job of repairn' his saddle."

Caught off guard, Jake tried to collect his thoughts. "You mean you went ridin'?"

"Yep, checked it out pretty close. Looks like it needs some ropin' done on it."

"Dad, I think you better slow down a little. You're not ready for all that yet."

"The hell I ain't. There's no time to waste anymore. I feel strong as a February Stud."

"At least wait 'till Sam gives you the results of the MRI."

"Fine, but I'm gonna' ride everyday 'till I get 'em. I need to get some strength back in this old cuerpo."

Levi continued to rope the practice dummy and rode almost everyday trying to develop his strength.

The next week they were back in the hospital.—"Anybody in this office?"

"Come in...come in. How are things at the ranch?"

"Everything seems to be goin' to plan. Dad's bustin' his ass actin' like a twenty year old."

"Got to hand it to him, Jake; he's determined."

"That's for damn sure, Brother."

"Listen you two, I don't need any uphill from y'all. If I'm gonna' do this I need your backin' one hundred percent."

"We're with you, Dad. We just don't want you to over do it."

"Your MRI looked very promising. The muscle and tendon transplants have healed unbelievably well."

"What do you think his capabilities are at this point?"

Levi looked at Jake. "It means I'm good to go."

"Yes, I'd say Dad is physically capable of resuming his normal activities. However, if you experience anything abnormal call me immediately."

"Verna and I will be coming out to see you as soon as I can get some time off from this place."

"That sounds good to us. We look forward to seein' you." Jake looked at Levi. "What you think? Should we get ourselves back to the ranch?"

Levi nodded. "I got work to do... Sam I don't have the words to thank you for all you've done for me... goes for you too, Jake. If you and Zeb hadn't got me outta that arroyo I'd have been coyote bait."

"You're the only Dad we have. Jake and I'd be lost without you to chew us out."

Jake shook his head. "That's the God's truth."

"I sure love you boys."

Sam waved at them. "Be careful going home."

Morning chores completed, Zeb and Levi gathered six head of calves and put them in the crowding pen by the roping chute. Levi then rode into the arena and warmed up the blood bay gelding.

"Benny's lookin' pretty fit isn't he?"

"I've been tryin' to condition him a little. He's always been one of the best horses I ever rode."

"Well if you don't tie a calf it won't be his fault, that's for sure."

"Go ahead and load 'em up and we'll see if all the practice is doin' any good."

Zeb opened the gate into the chute as Pedro and Pata nipped at the calve's heels, pushing them forward. Levi loped Benny in a circle swinging his rope, then rode into the box.

"Let 'im go."

The calf darted forward, hitting a full run. Levi checked the gelding, then lunged forward. Benny had him in position before Levi could get his timing and his loop hit the running calf on the shoulder. "Whew! That little son of a bitch was fast."

"All of these Longhorn calves are fast. You gotta get used to 'em. Calves at these rodeos today are fresh, fast and big."

"Guess your right."

Levi stepped off Benny and checked his cinch, then led him over to the chute.

"Maybe I can get Andy to use that video camera on my runs so I can see what I'm doin' wrong."

"That's a damn good idea. He's not in school tomorrow. You can ask him tonight. Meantime, you better go ahead and run these a couple times. Just try to get your timing down and don't worry so much about catchin' real fast. Your speed will pick up once you get to catchin'."

"You're right. Maybe I'm just try'n to move too fast. I'll just try to get in position and time up better before I throw."

The two cow dogs pushed another calf into the chute as Zeb closed the end gate. Levi walked Benny into the box, turned him around, and backed him into the corner. The blood bay's ears were pointed as his eyes fixed on the calf in the chute. Levi nodded, and the calf jumped forward. Benny hesitated a second and again bounded forward quickly, putting his roper in perfect position. Levi swung his rope, timing it up with the running calf and made the delivery, catching the calf cleanly around the neck. The blood bay cut an eleven as Levi dismounted on the run, working his way down the rope, quickly flanking and tying the calf. Then he walked back, got on his horse and nudged him forward.

Zeb was there to take the pigging string off and release the calf.

"Hey, that looked pretty damn good. You had him timed up just right."

"Thanks. Guess my nerves settled a little that go-round."

"Keep that up and you'll be smokin' 'em pretty soon."

"I sure hope so. We need the dinero."

"Are you feelin' okay?"

"Yeah. It just seems strange ropin' like this again. It's been many a moon since I've done this. It's a different feelin' from draggin' calves to the iron."

"I'll bet so. That ol' adrenaline is probably kickin' in pretty hard. Your old days on the road are comin' out."

"How many's that Zeb?"

"You've made eight runs and tied five."

"We'd better call it a day. Benny and I need a breather. We'll try it again tomorrow."

They turned the calves back into the trap and walked toward the barn, leading the calf horse. Pedro and Pata made their way to the barn first and started drinking from a water trough.

Levi looked at Zeb. "Give me your honest opinion— do you think I'll do okay on the road?"

"I think it's pretty early to really know for sure, but if you keep improvin' you'll do okay. To be honest with you I didn't think you'd be able to do what you did today. But you improved on every run. That's sayin' a lot. Once you think you're ready I think you should hit a few smaller rodeos around here. If you do okay—and I think you will—move up to some better payin' rodeos. Hell, you still got a Gold Card so you can make about any size show you want to."

"Thanks, Zeb. I truly appreciate the help you've given me. You're the best compadre a man could ask for."

Zeb grinned. "Thanks, Levi. I'll remind you of that when you start cashin' some checks."

They both chuckled and walked to the barn.

Chapter 28

"Howdy, Granddad. How'd the practice go today?"

"Fair for the first time. I was havin' timing problems at first, but it seemed to get better as I roped. Zeb told me you might not have school tomorrow."

"That's right. The teachers are havin' meetings of some kind. I'm gonna hang out around here. Maybe work with one of those colts."

"Could I ask a favor of you?" Levi asked.

"Sure... what do you need?"

"That camera you got."

"You mean my video camera?" Andy replied.

"Yeah, the video camera. I was wonderin' if you could use it on me while I'm makin' my runs?"

"Sure, Granddad. I'd love to do that. Maybe I could use the film for a project in my Ag. class. Mr. Adams likes us to bring in different things like that. I'll be ready tomorrow whenever you are."

"Thanks, Andy. I think it'll help me a lot to see what I'm doin' wrong. Hopefully it will help me improve."

"What you two outlaws plottin'?"

"I was just tellin' Andy how my ropin' went today."

"Yeah, and he wants me to film his practice tomorrow."

"I was thinkin' it might help me see what I'm doin' wrong so I can correct it."

"Not a bad idea. How did it go today?"

"Like I was tellin' Andy, it went fair for the first time on horseback. I rode Benny and he helped me a lot. He puts you where you need to be."

"He's a good one for sure. Wish I could have watched you today, but I wanted to go over and see how Javier was doin' with the two three year olds. I'll give you a hand tomorrow for sure."

"Thanks, Jake. I'd appreciate that and I'm sure Zeb would too. I 'bout wore him out today."

The next day, Levi saddled Benny as the others put the calves in the crowding pen.

"How do you think he did yesterday?"

"Not bad. He was a little off but the more runs he made the better things went for him."

"Did he hold up okay?"

"He was ready to call it a day by the time he made his last run."

"I sure hope he didn't over do it."

"It's gonna be hard to hold him back now. His mind's set on goin' down the road."

Levi rode into the arena. "Looks like you two have 'em ready. Where's Andy?"

"He'll be here in just a minute. He went to the house to get a couple more tapes."

A few minutes later Andy walked into the arena. "I'm ready, Granddad. I'll get about three-quarters down the arena so I can get you comin' out and trackin' the calf before you catch 'im. That should make a pretty good shot for you to study."

"Sounds good to me."

Zeb opened the roping chute as the cow dogs nipped at the hocks and pushed the calves forward. Zeb closed the end gate and the first calf was ready for the roper. Levi backed Benny into the box. The blood bay was all business.

Levi nodded and the chute sprang open. Benny quickly had Levi in position and the loop passed over the calf's head. Levi pitched his slack like a pro and hit the ground on the run, quickly flanking and tying the calf. He stood and walked back to the gelding, mounted him and nudged him forward, giving the calf some slack.

Jake took off the pigging string and released the bawling calf. Walking up to his dad, he looked up and handed him the pigging string. "Damn, that looked real good. That'll be one to watch a couple of times."

Levi yelled over to Andy. "Did you get it?"

"Sure did, Granddad. It was excitin'."

Levi rode back up to the chute.

Zeb grinned. "Damn, that was the best run you've made. Guess all you needed was to have it bein' filmed."

"That's enough outta you. I just want to get on the right track as best I can."

"Well, it looks like you're doin' that."

He made a few more runs catching every calf he ran. "Guess that'll do for today, boys. Thanks for all your help."

"Hell, Dad, we wouldn't a missed it. You roped damn good."

"Yeah, I ain't seen 'im rope like that in thirty years."

Andy ran up to them. "Boy, Granddad that was great! I got it all on tape too."

Jake looked at Levi. "Dad, do you think you're up to the stress of goin' down the road?"

"It's like this: I haven't felt this good in a long time. My ropin' is pickin' up. I believe I can give 'em a run for their money at the smaller rodeos. I'd like to hit some Old Timer Rodeos too, maybe see some of the old crew at the same time. Never know... I might make the Old Timer Finals."

"That's some pretty impressive plans, seein' as how you've gone through some pretty rough times over the last couple of months."

"I know, but I'd like to make a run at it. We could use some extra money around here if I can rope well enough. Besides I owe it to Randy."

"Dad if you think that's what you got to do you have my backin' one hundred percent."

"Thanks, Jake. I need that more than you can imagine."

Jake gave his Dad a hug. "You go get 'em, cowboy."

The dualie was loaded with a couple of duf-
fle bags of clean clothes, and Benny was in the
trailer, ready to take Levi to the pay window.

"Come on, Zeb. We better get goin'.
Weatherford's a pretty good drive."

"Hold on. Kathy's bringin' us out a basket of
fried chicken. I don't want you to starve us to
death."

The pickup headed down the dusty road,
the two old cowboys silent in deep anticipation of
what lay ahead. They turned onto Highway 35 and
headed north to Weatherford. When they hit Bel-
ton they stopped for fuel.

"I'll check Benny while you throw in some
diesel."

"Okay, Levi. Hey you remember this country?"

"How could I forget it? Just down the road
there is our old stompin' grounds... Guada-Killeen.
Man, those were some days weren't they?"

"That's no damn lie. Did you ever think
we'd make it this far?"

"I wasn't sure of anything back then."

That evening they pulled into the rodeo
grounds and unload Benny, then bedded him down
and made their way to a motel. They were at the
rodeo grounds the next morning by six-thirty,

feeding Benny and cleaning his stall. Finishing up, they headed for a café.

"What can I get you this morning?"

"Go ahead, Zeb."

"Okay, I'll have two eggs over easy, hash browns, sausage and coffee."

"How about you, cowboy?"

Levi looked up at the portly waitress. "I'll have the same."

"You want cream with your coffee?"

"Look at us— what's your first guess?"

"Guess that was a stupid question. I'll be right back with your coffee."

"What the hell's wrong with you today, Levi? She was just tryin' to be nice."

"Guess I'm just a little nervous."

She brought back the coffee and set it on the table. "Your order will be up in a few."

"Ma'am, I want to apologize for bein' so rude."

"Thank you Sir, I won't spit on your eggs now." She turned and walked off.

"She's sure a sassy one."

"You might've had it coming."

Levi inspected his eggs as she put his plate on the table. She grinned. "Don't worry; you're safe."

"Thanks, ma'am."

They finished breakfast and headed back to the rodeo grounds.

After checking Benny's water, they decided to walk over and check out the draw.

"Looks like you're fourth to go."

"Yeah, and there's only seven in the go-round. Glad I didn't have to rope in the slack this mornin'."

"Yeah, you'd rather have it out with a chunky waitress. Good thing you apologized. That heifer could have rolled you up in her shirt tail and farted your brains out."

With a slight chuckle, Levi replied, "Yeah, she was about five axe handles broad across the ass wasn't she?"

"She could've got plumb rank for sure, Levi."

The grandstands begin to fill as the announcer began to warm up the crowd. "Welcome, folks. The rodeo committee asked me to thank all of you for helping make this a great event. If you will please stand for *'The National Anthem'* while our queen and her court post the colors... thank you very much. If you can hear the chutes rattlin' it's because they're loadin' the bareback horses for our first event. The first bareback rider is Chance Carlton from Waco. He'll be ridin' Digger out of chute number one."

The bronc snorted as he leaped out of the chute, kicking high and bucking straight across the arena, then turning back toward the fence as a horn blared, ending the eight-seconds of bone jarring misery. The crowd cheered as the pick up men helped Chance off the bronc. The announcer came on again. "Let's see how our judges scored that ride. Not too bad. A 78. Might get him to the pay window."

Levi saddled Benny and got ready as the announcer continued to work his way through the bareback riders until the last rider walked out of the arena.

"The next event will be the tie down roping. You may have heard it called calf roping in the past. We have some pretty tough ropers with us today, so let's get to it. The first roper out today is BJ Sanders from Cleburn. He's been roping consistently this year."

The calf left the chute. He was a hard-running calf, BJ caught him three-quarters of the way down the arena for a time of eleven point four-seconds.

"That was a hard running calf folks, just the luck of the draw. The next roper is Harvey Brown from Stephenville." Harvey, called for the calf and had him roped in eight-seconds flat. "Nice run. Give that cowboy a big hand."

"Riding into the arena now is Sam Martin from Denton. The time for him to beat is eight-seconds flat." Sam called for the calf, and pushed the barrier and roped his calf in seven point eight-seconds. "Give that cowboy a hand. He just set the new time to beat. Nice job. Our next cowboy is Levi Blevins. He's from a ranch down in the hill country. Levi hasn't competed in rodeo for a number of years, but I understand he's been spending a lot of time in the practice pen."

Levi rode into the arena and loped the blood bay gelding in a tight circle in front of the box, then walked him in, turned him around and backed into the corner. Benny's ears pointed, his eyes fixed on the chute. Levi nodded and the calf sprang forward as the chute opened.

The gelding and Levi moved together as though they knew it was for all the marbles. Benny had his partner in position, giving him a perfect throw for a clean catch, and the gelding set up, cutting an eleven turning the calf toward Levi, backing just enough to keep the rope tight. Levi fluidly moved down the rope, flanking and tying the calf with expert precision. He stood and walked back to the gelding, stepped up and nudged him forward, giving the calf the required slack. He sat and waited as the crew reached down and untied his pigging string and released the calf. The arena hand handed up his pigging string. "Great run, Sir."

"Folks here it is. Seven point two-seconds! Now there's a cowboy, folks. Not only has he set the time to beat, but he's the oldest contestant in the entire rodeo. Great job, Levi! That was something to witness."

The crowd burst into cheers as Levi rode out of the arena, tipping his hat.

Zeb walked up to him as he rode toward the trailer. "That was one of the damn-dest things

I've seen in a Month of Sundays! I haven't seen you move that fast since you got caught kissin' that captain's girlfriend in 44. If you keep ropin' like that you'll have enough dinero to burn a herd a wet cows."

Levi got off his horse, loosened the cinch, took the bridle off and haltered him.

"I'm gonna cool 'im out a little." He turned and led the blood bay toward an open area. Zeb stood there watching his old friend as he walked away. "What's got into him?"

In the distance, the announcer called for the next roper. "Dell Sharp from Waco is the roper. Dell's sitting first in the non-pro circuit. He's a former intercollegiate champion."

He called for the calf. Seconds later, cheers from the crowd rose above the grandstand.

"What a run! Folks this roping is getting tougher than a two-dollar flank steak. Dell's time was seven-point one seconds, putting him in the lead. Give him a big hand, folks. That's the winning time for the tie-down roping Levi Blevins is second with a seven-two."

The last bull rider had just been whipped around like a rag doll as the rodeo came to an end.

"Folks, thank you for making this years rodeo one of the best. We'll see you next year when you'll once again see some of the best cowboys in the country compete for cash, buckles and bragging rights. Drive carefully going home."

Levi and Zeb loaded Benny and drove out of the rodeo grounds headed for home. Levi asked, "Are you hungry?"

"I could eat the south end of a north bound skunk."

Levi pulled into a truck stop. "We'll get some fuel and grab a steak. Whaddya' say?"

"Thought you'd never ask."

They sat at the table talking as they chowed down on a prime piece of beef.

"That was one hell of a start, Levi. You were ropin' against some toughs."

"Yep... went pretty good I guess, but I was second. That's dinero left on the table."

"Yeah, but you still brought home some bacon."

They finished their steaks and headed for home driving down I-35.

"I want you to know somethin', Zeb said. I'm proud of the way you handled yourself today. Hell, man you roped against fellas more than half your age and beat all but one of 'em, and he's sittin' first in the non-pro circuit."

"Thanks, partner, I appreciate that. Comin' from you it means a lot."

"Tell me, how do you feel physically? I mean I haven't seen you move like that in years."

"Let me tell you somethin'. Since Sam operated on me I've been experiencing some strange things. It's like I'm twenty years old again. I don't

251

have the muscle pain or other physical problems I had. I feel like I could wip the world."

"Okay, here's the big one Levi: how's the Major and his Twin Captains doin'?"

"It's like this pard. Next time we go to the Lonely Bull, those coeds better keep their knees together 'cause I feel like a February stud most of the time."

"Guess you can give me your blue pills since you won't need 'em anymore."

"Not a problem."

Pulling off I-35 they hit the dusty dirt road leading back to the ranch.

Levi pulled up next to the barn.

"Guess we fooled 'em again. I'm beat."

He unloaded the gelding led him into the barn, and put him in a stall.

"I'll get you some hay and grain, Benny. You did a hell of a job today. You're one hell of a horse."

"Come in Zeb you're just in time for some breakfast."

"Thanks, Kathy. I really could use it this mornin'. That drive home seemed to take forever last night. Anything excitin' happen while we were gone?"

"Not really. Just the same old sixes and sevens."

Levi walked in. "What's goin' on this mornin'?"

"Not a lot, Dad. We were just waitin' to hear how you did." Jake said.

"It went pretty fair, we had a good time."

"It went better than pretty fair," Zeb said. "He roped like a champion."

"Come on now, Zeb. It wasn't all that great."

"Let me tell y'all about it. He out-roped all but one of 'em, and that one's sittin' first in the non-pro circuit. Your Dad handled himself like a pro. He won close to nineteen hundred dollars. That's not bad on a hundred dollar entry... two and a half tanks of fuel, and a truck stop steak. I'd like to be able to do that a couple times a month."

"Sounds pretty good, Dad. Hell, second is pretty good for your first time out."

"It went okay, I recon'."

"What you got planned now?"

"I've been thinkin' about goin' down the road a little."

"You think your up to it, Dad?"

Levi nodded. "Sure do, there's too much ridin' on it."

"If you think that's what you need to do, more power to you. We'll keep things goin' around here."

Jake looked over at Zeb. "You better tag along with him. He's gonna need some company. 'Sides, somebody's got to control his skirt chasin'."

"Hell, Jake, you don't want to ruin all the fun, do you?"

Zeb ginned. "He's right. We don't want you blowin' all your winnins' on some buckle bunny."

"That'll be the day."

"When do you think you'll pull out?"

"Think we'll hit the road tomorrow afternoon. There's a three-day rodeo in Abilene startin' Friday. Should be some money there."

Andy and Jake helped them get the dualie loaded as they prepared to head down the road. Everyone is there as they put the final supplies in the back seat.

"Guess we better get on the road."

"If you need anything out there give us a call."

"Don't worry; we will for sure."

Kathy walked over and gave them each a hug and peck on the cheek. "Now you two behave yourselves."

Sally kissed Zeb on the cheek. "You take care of my Grandpa."

"Don't worry, Honey. I sure will."

They all waved as the two old cowboys pulled out. "See you later.'

Friday morning they drove into Abilene and headed for the rodeo grounds.

"How you feelin'?"

"Pretty good. I'll just be glad to get this one behind me."

"Don't sweat it. Just do the best you can, an' everything'll come out in the wash."

They walked over to the office to check the schedule. Zeb said, "Looks like some of the same boys that were in Weatherford will be here."

"Sure does. Dell Sharp's up on Sunday."

"Don't let that bother you. He puts his pants on just like you do, one leg at a time. Keep your mind on things and you'll do fine. He could screw up easy as not."

"Hell, I'm the last roper up on Sunday. Guess I'll know what I have to beat."

"Yeah, an it'll give us some time to cool out."

"Let's go over and check Benny. Maybe I'll lunge him a little, then we can take in the slack, I'd like to see how the calf ropers do."

"He's lookin' pretty loose."

"Yeah, I thought that ride would have him pretty stiff. He's well conditioned so I don't think we'll have any trouble with 'im tyin' up."

Levi lunged him for a while, then he and Zeb walked over to the arena to watch some of the calf roping.

"That wasn't a bad run. Eight-five might hold up this go 'round."

"If that's the best time turned in you should do okay here."

"Let's not get too cocky. There's a lot of ropers here."

As they sat at the back of the chute watching the roping, Zeb heard a familiar voice behind him. "Hey cowboy, what you doing here?"

He turned to see Ruth standing there looking up at him. "Well I'll be damned! What brings you up here?"

"One of my friends from school came up to watch her boy friend rope. What are you two doing here?"

"Levi, decided to start calf ropin' again, so we're goin' down the road a little."

"Are you roping too?"

"Na not me, I just came along to keep 'im outa' trouble. Oh excuse me... Levi, you remember Ruth here, don't you?"

"How could I forget a pretty gal like her? How you doin', Miss?"

"The question is how are *you* doing? You were in the hospital the last time I saw you, and if I remember correctly you were in a bad way."

"Yeah, a lot has happened since then."

"I'll tell you about it later," Zeb said. "You're a sight for sore eyes. How is school goin' for you?"

"We just have a couple more months and I should graduate."

"That's great, Ruth. I'll bet you'll be glad to finish up."

"That's an understatement."

"You say you're here to watch someone rope? Who is it?"

"My friend's been dating a roper from Waco named Dell Sharp. Do you know him?"

Levi got a startled look on his face. "Yeah, a little. He's a pretty fair hand."

"What are you two doing later?"

Zeb looked over at Levi. "Don't have anything really planned."

"Why don't you meet us at the Red Barn? It's not the Lonely Bull, but they have a good band. I'll introduce you to some of the gals and you and I can do some two stepping."

Zeb looked over at Levi. "What you say, pard? Maybe the Major would like to meet one of 'em?"

"Is there someone else here with y'all? Who's the Major?"

"Nah, we're here alone," Zeb said. "We just joke around about the Major, huh Levi?"

"Well, why don't I meet you there around eight?"

"Sounds good, Ruth."

Zeb hopped down and gave her a bear hug and a peck on the cheek. "See you at eight."

"Sounds good. See you later, Levi."

"See you, Ruth."

"What you think 'bout that?"

"The Major huh? You're gonna get me cut for sure."

After the last bull rider was ironed out, they headed over to take care of Benny and make their way back to the motel to clean up.

Zeb said, "That Red Barn is just down the road a little. I remember seein' it when we went down to the Waffle Barn."

As they pulled into the parking lot, it was hard for them to find a place to park the dualie. "Man this place is hoppin'. She sure knew what she was talkin' about."

Finding a spot they got out and headed into the honky tonk. Ruth spotted them and walked over to get them. "Sure glad you made it. We have seats for you at our table. I'll introduce you to everyone."

As they walked to the table Levi spotted Dell Sharp sitting there with a nice looking redhead.

"Everyone, this is Zeb Pike and Levi Blevins. Fellas, this is Nancy Bell, Carol Samuels and this couple is Peggy Shepard and Dell Sharp."

"We're pleased to meet y'all."

"Well, sit down–Zeb you sit here next to me. I don't want you wonderin' off."

Dell Sharp looked over at Levi. "You took second at Weatherford. That was a hell of a run you made. Had to bust my ass to beat you. See you're up after me Sunday."

Sensing a certain amount of animosity he looked at Dell with a squint in his eye. "That's the way it looks."

Sensing friction, Ruth looked over at Zeb. "How about a dance?"

"Why shore', little lady. I thought you'd never ask." She chuckled as he walked her out on the dance floor.

Levi looked over at the pretty little brunette, How'd you like to dance, Nancy?"

"Sure, I'd love to."

After Levi and Nancy left the table, Dell said, "Come on Peggy, let's dance. That old man thinks he's somethin'. Come Sunday I'm gonna show him how to rope."

"What's wrong with you, Dell?"

"I just don't like bein' pushed by someone his age."

The night wore on with dancing, laughter and hard core drinking. The old cowboys showed the gals they didn't need a rocking chair.

Ruth whispered, "Zeb, I got a room over at the Westerner. It has a coffee pot and the coffee shop serves a good breakfast."

Not needing any further invitation he looked at Levi. "You're on your own, pard."

Zeb and Ruth got up and walked out. Levi sat there looking around, not really wanting to be there any longer with the belligerent Dell Sharp. Nancy looked over at Levi. "Looks like I need to find a ride and a place to stay." Totally saturated with tequila, Dell attempted to accommodate her. "You...you can stay...with us."

"Actually, I was wondering if Levi would help me out."

He looked over at the pretty young cowgirl. "What? Why sure, Nancy." Without any further urging Levi escorted her out to the dualie.

The next morning Zeb pulled up to the stalls in a new Mercedes.

Levi grinned. "Damn! Where'd you steal that?"

"Ruth was feelin' a little hung over so I borrowed her car keys, an' they fit this un'."

"Yeah, I left mine at the motel too. These gals today just can't keep up."

He continued to brush the gelding. "Man, that little gal could've started a forest fire last night."

"I take it the Major stood at attention most of the night puttin' out the flames."

"You might say that. How'd those blue pills work for you?"

"Well you know that ad that says if you experience a four-hour erection to call a doctor? Well the phone was dead."

"Hell of a note, Zeb."

"Looks like you got things pretty much caught up here. Why don't we meet y'all at that little cafe next to the motel?"

"Sounds good."

The couples sat and enjoyed breakfast over some lively conversation. Levi said, "That was some pretty good chow. What y'all want to do now?"

Ruth smiled. "We hate to leave good company, but we have some girl things to do."

Zeb looked at her. "What sorta' girl things?"

"Go shopping."

"Oh. Well, guess we'll see y'all later then."

Zeb and Levi crawled into the dualie and drove back to the rodeo grounds to take in the calf roping. "Hell it looks like the times to beat are in the mid-eights. If they keep this up you can pick up a check."

"Let's hope so."

"I think I'll take care of Benny and head back to the room and rest awhile."

"That sounds good. Think I'll tag along"

The next morning Levi scratched his head. "Man, I must'a been tired. I couldn't wake up last night. We'd better get over and feed Benny. He's prob'ly wonderin' what happened to us."

He led the blood bay over to the trailer and saddled him. In the distance the announcer was announcing the bareback competition. Levi selected a rope and swung it, roping the dummy a couple of times, then led the gelding toward the roping chute.

One calf roper after another was announced. "Looks like our ropers are havin' some problems today," the announcer said. "Yesterday's time of eight-four is the time to beat. Dell Sharp is up next. He's sitting first in the non-pro standings."

Dell backed his horse into the box and nodded for the calf. It broke fast and cut left as Dell tried to catch it and time up. He threw and the loop went around the calf's head and one leg. He got to the calf and struggled with the tie. Disgust was written all over his face as he walked back to his horse. As he rode up the calf struggled and kicked loose from the pigging string. The flagger rode up, waving the flag. "That's sure a surprise folks," the announcer said. "Dell will get a no time." Dell rode out of the arena and past Levi staring straight ahead trying not to acknowledge him.

"Our final calf roper is Levi Blevins. Levi's back on the circuit again and doing well. He's been out of competition for quite a spell."

Levi rode into the box and backed the gelding. He nodded his head and the calf drove forward. The blood bay was at the barrier as it popped back, a clean break. Levi swung twice and put the loop over the calf's head, the gelding did his job perfectly. Levi ran down the rope and flanked the calf, then made a clean tie. He walked back, stepped up and gave the calf some slack. "There it is folks a new fast time seven-nine. That's your winner in the calf roping. Nice job Levi!"

Levi rode out of the arena and tipped his hat as the crowd roared.

Zeb met him as he rode out. "Damn, Levi you really put it on em'! That Dell Sharp already loaded up and lit out a here like a scalded cat. You'd a thought he shit his pants or somethin'. Hell, I think he even went off and forgot that red head."

Levi stepped off Benny and loosened the cinch, then patted him on the neck as he led him back to the stall. "Well let's cool Benny out and head to Amarillo."

"Sounds good to me. That should be a good ropin' for you."

He rode into the Amarillo arena. "Folks this cowboy has been red hot. He took a second in Weatherford, and last week he won the calf roping in Abilene. I understand he had an almost fatal horse wreck at his ranch, but he seems to be back with us in full force. And get this: he's the oldest cowboy competing here."

Levi backed Benny into the box. Again they were poised for the run. Levi nodded and the calf broke out of the chute. Benny got Levi in shape as he delivered the loop after making two swings. Benny set the calf up and Levi moved with precision, tying the calf securely.

Levi rode out of the arena as the announcer gave his time. "Read it and weep, calf ropers. That seven-nine on the timer just won the calf roping."

The young ropers looked at their competition as he rode out of the arena. One of them shook his head as the old cowboy rode by. "That old fart will burn you."

Another roper replied, "Would you ever believe it?"

Levi rode over to the trailer and unsaddled.

Zeb grinned broadly. "Damn partner, you done it again. What's got into you?"

Levi, still focused, just replied, "We'd better get on the road pretty soon. I'm up in El Paso tomorrow night."

Pointing the dualie down 385, Zeb looked over at his old partner. "You're really startin' to get their attention."

"I don't cotton much to attention. I'm just interested in payin' medical bills and sendin' dinero back to the ranch. What I've put the family through is hard for me to bare. All I can hope for is to keep it goin' long enough to square things up."

Zeb looked at Levi. "You feelin' alright?"

"Most of the time. Here lately there's days I get pretty tuckered out."

"Think you better take a break? You've been pushin' it pretty hard."

"Nah, I think I'm good to go."

"Damn it, if you're not doin' well you better tell me. You remember what Sam told you?"

"You'll be the first to know if I start goin' down hill."

They hit I-20, at Odessa and pulled in for some fuel. "Think I'll stretch my legs a little while you fill er' up."

Levi walked back and checked Benny, and walked away slowly. Zeb watched him, shook his head and began to fuel up the dualie.

At four–thirty in the morning they pulled into the Colosseum. "I'll find a place to put Benny. You kick back, Levi."

"Thanks, pard."

Levi leaned the seat back to catch some shuteye and was snoring away in just a few seconds.

Zeb found an empty panel corral and put the gelding in, then threw him a flake of hay, filled the water bucket and tied it to a panel. "That ought to keep you for awhile."

He walked around, finally found a pay phone and placed a collect call back to the ranch. "Mornin,' Jake. Oh it's goin' pretty good. He won at Amarillo, and now we're here in El Paso. Yeah that's what I'm callin' about. No, nothin' serious. He's just gettin' tired. He's in the pickup restin' right now. If it gets any worse I'll bring 'im home. Give our best to everyone. Okay, we'll talk at you later."

Zeb walked back and checked the gelding, and then walked to the dualie. Levi was sawing logs. Zeb got in to get a little rest.

Still feeling drained, Levi sat on the gelding behind the roping chute. "Levi Blevins is your next roper, the announcer said. "This cowboy comes to us from the Hill Country. He's been doing pretty good since getting back on the road. He's won the last two ropings he's been to."

Levi rode into the box and set the gelding, then nodded his head. Getting out clean he roped and tied the calf in seven-five.

"There you have it folks. Another great time turned in by Levi. Let's show him we appreciate him."

Cheers and rebel yells came from the crowd as he left the arena.

Riding out to the trailer, he slowly got off and stood next to Benny, holding the saddle horn to maintain himself.

Zeb looked at him closely. "What's goin' on, Levi? You okay?"

Unable to speak, Levi handed his old partner the reins, staggered over and sat on the trailer fender. Finally he caught his breath. "Don't know, Zeb. That last run took it out of me pretty bad."

Zeb hesitated. "Well, I didn't tell you this, but I called Jake this mornin'."

"What the hell did you do that for?"

"Cause I'm worried as hell 'bout you, that's why. You've been pushin' yourself too hard. Hell, those kids couldn't keep up with the pace you've set."

"I need to bring in more dinero."

"Hell, man you've won two in a row with a second in another'n' an' prob'ly got this'n in the bag. That's pretty damn good any way you figure it."

"You're right. Maybe I'd better get back to the ranch for a spell."

"I'll get Benny taken care of, and call Jake to tell him we're comin' home. You rest a little. When I get back we'll hit the road. We can be to the ranch this time tomorrow."

Chapter 29

It was late afternoon when Jake and Andy rode in. "Look Dad, Benny is in his pen."

"They must'a got back while we were checkin' cows. Let's get unsaddled and get up to the house."

Walking into the front room they saw the tired old cowboy sitting in his recliner, his face drawn with fatigue. "Howdy, Dad" Jake said. "It's good to see you. How was the trip?"

Levi looked up at them with a half-hearted grin. "Ah, it was okay."

Jake asked, "Where's Zeb?"

"I Think he's in the kitchen with Kathy, getting us some coffee."

"How's the ropin' goin', Granddad?"

"Not bad. I hit a lick or two. Just had to take a little break."

Jake walked over and sat down next to his dad. "Tell me the truth. What's goin' on with you?"

"Don't rightly know, I was feelin' real good. Then I sorta hit a wall up in Amarillo. Then in El Paso the next day I just sorta caved in. Couldn't seem to navigate very well... completely ran outta steam by the time I roped."

Jake got up and walked toward the phone. "I'm gonna call Sam and see what he suggests. He'll probably want you to come in."

"Hello Sam, Yeah they're back. He looks pretty worn out. Okay, we'll do that. Thanks, Sam. 'Bye." He set down the phone and walked back into the living room.

"What'd he say?"

"He wants you there day after tomorrow at eight in the mornin'. You're not to eat anything after ten tomorrow night, just water. He said he'd be drawing blood and checkin' you out."

Levi stared at the wall. "Hell here we go again."

"It won't be all that bad. You've been through worse."

Trying to change the subject, Levi said, "How are he and Verna doin'? Have you seen them lately?"

"As a matter of fact they've been out a couple of times. They seem to be doin' a lot better. She and Kathy have even been doin' some quiltin'."

"I'm damn glad to hear that. Maybe things are workin' out for 'em."

"It sure looks like it to us. When she and Kathy are together workin' on quilts they act like sisters."

"That's wonderful. That debutante needed some down home skills." He looked over at his Grandson sitting there quietly. "How's the calvin' comin' along?"

"Real good. We've already calved out seventy-nine head. We haven't had to pull one yet."

"Damn, that sounds pretty good. We usually have to pull one or two by now. You're doin' real good, Andy."

The young cowboy looked down at the floor. "Yeah, but we'd a prob'ly done better if Randy was here to help."

Zeb and Kathy walked in with a tray of mugs brimming with hot C. "Ready for some coffee and pie, Levi?"

"Thought you'd never get here."

Levi slowly walked into the hospital, Jake beside him holding his arm. "I thought my days comin' to this place were finished."

"Sam will probably have you back on the road in no time."

"Sure hope so. I was feelin' pretty good out there."

"You ought to feel good. Hell, you sent close to eighty-five hundred home in little over a month. The way you were goin' you might a made the finals."

"Wouldn't that a been a hoot? That really would've pissed those youngsters off."

"I'm not sure about that Dad. I think you got a lot of respect from what we read in the ropin' news."

Samuel walked up to them as they made their way down the hallway toward his office. "Just who I'm looking for. It's good to see both of you. What's up with this champion calf roper?"

"Good to see you too, Sam. I brought you somethin'."

Reaching into his vest pocket he pulled out a box and handed it to Samuel.

"What's this?"

"Just somethin' I found up in Amarillo."

He opened the box and pulled out a sterling silver buckle inlaid with gold letters. "Wow, Dad, I can't accept this. You worked hard for it."

"Benny did most of the work; I just went along for the ride. Just want you to have somethin' that will remind you of what you and Randy did for me."

Sam looked at the silver buckle in his hands. "This will truly be cherished. Thanks Dad."

They walked into his office and sat down. "Tell me what's going on with you."

After Levi explained how he'd been feeling Sam said, "Okay, I've arranged for some lab work and a CAT-scan for today." He picked up the phone. "Please have an orderly bring a wheel chair to my office. I have a patient that needs to go to the lab. Thank you." He hung up. "They'll be right here."

"What you think's goin' on with me, Sam?"

"I'm not sure. Once I get the test results, I'll have a better idea. I'm going to order an EKG and we may need another MRI. I just want to cover as many bases as I can."

The orderly arrived and they helped Levi into the wheelchair. "Take him down to the lab and wait for him. We'll need to get him over for a CAT-scan when they're through drawing blood and getting an EKG."

"Okay Doctor, I'll stay with him. Levi and I have had some interesting times around here."

"Dad, we'll get with you when all the tests are completed."

"Thanks, Son."

Samuel picked up the phone and placed a call to the lab technician. "This is Doctor Blevins. I want a rush put on his blood work. I need the results ASAP. I sent orders for an EKG with the orderly. Page me if you need to. I'll be in the cafeteria." He hung up the phone and looked at Jake. "What you say we get some coffee?"

The brothers walked toward the cafeteria. "I'm going to admit him. He needs to be here first thing in the morning. If you don't mind, I'd like for you to stay at our house tonight."

The next day came fast. "Good morning," Sam said. "What do you two have going this morning?"

"Not a hell of a lot. Jake was just tellin' me he had a nice visit with you and Verna last night."

Jake grinned at Sam. "I was tellin' him about that lobster she fixed for supper. Man that was tasty!"

Levi looked at him like he was crazy. "I'm a steak and potato man. I don't cotton to eatin' bugs."

"Ah Dad, you don't know what you're missing," Sam said. "When you get out of here we'll have you over for a nice lobster dinner."

"You better have some beef to go long with it."

The orderly arrived with the wheelchair to take him to get the MRI. "I hope to hell this all ends soon. I'm gettin' tired of this crap. See you later, boys."

When the orderly had wheeled him out, Sam said, "Jake, I think you better take him back to the ranch when we finish the MRI. He needs a lot of rest and he'll do much better out there. He hates this place. I'll call you once I've studied all the test results."

"What you thinks goin' on, Sam?"

"I just don't know yet."

The orderly wheeled Levi in. "Well here he is. They're all finished with him."

"That damn thing sure is noisy. It's like bein' in a fifty-five gallon drum with someone hittin' it with a ball-peen hammer."

Jake said, "I'll get the car."

He pulled up to the curb and the orderly helped Levi in. "We'll see you later Mr. Blevins."

"I hope to hell not."

They got to the ranch about three-thirty in the afternoon. Levi slept most of the way out.

Jake said, "How you doin' Dad?"

"Just can't seem to get rested up."

"Let's get you in the house. Maybe you need to lie down for awhile."

"Sounds good to me."

Levi laid down and fell into a deep sleep, not waking until morning.

Kathy was in the kitchen fixing breakfast when he slowly walked in. "Mornin', Pop. Did you sleep well?"

"I was out like Lotty's eye. Don't think I wrinkled the covers much."

"Jake said they put you through the mill the last two days."

Jake walked in. "Well, looks like old Rip Van Winkle's back with us."

"That'll be 'nough outa you. How 'bout showin' me how those three year olds are doin' that Javier rode for us?"

"Sure. Finish up your breakfast and we'll go down and look 'em over."

Standing at the corral Levi watched Andy work the gray. "That boy sure is makin' a hand. He's sittin' that gray like he was born on 'im."

"Yeah, he sure loves ridin' 'im. When we got 'em back from Javier he'd put a handle on 'em like no one else."

"Hey Zeb, how's Benny doin'?"

"He's just waitin' on you."

Levi turned away from the corral and started toward Benny when suddenly his legs buckled out from under him. Jake and Zeb got there pronto to help him up. "You okay, Dad? What the hell happened?"

"I'm not sure. My legs just quit me."

"Let's get you to the house."

Jake and Zeb walked him into the house and sat him in the recliner. He looked at them with fear in his eyes. "Must'a lost my balance."

"I'm gonna call Sam."

"Hell, don't bother him. He's got more to do than worry 'bout me. I'll be fine."

"No, I'm gonna' call 'im."

Jake left to make the call while Zeb stayed with Levi. "What's goin' on with you? You're not yourself."

"I'm not sure... I just feel weak."

"Sam wants you back to the hospital as soon as we can get you there."

"What the hell did he say?"

"He just wants you in there. Help me get 'im in the pickup, Zeb. Let Kathy know where we are when she gets back."

"Sure, Jake. Levi, you be careful y'hear?"

Andy ran up as the pickup sped away. "What happened?"

"I don't rightly know. Levi fell so we helped him down here. Your Dad called Sam and he said to get him into the hospital pronto."

Jake wheeled into the emergency ramp, jumped out and ran in. "Will you help me get my dad in here?"

They pushed a gurney out and assisted Levi onto it. Samuel walked up as they pushed him through the doors. "Thanks for getting him here so quickly. Let's get him into emergency."

"What's goin' on, Sam?"

"Let's get him settled and we'll talk."

The emergency staff started an IV and placed him on a monitor and started oxygen.

"Jake, I need to speak with you privately."

"Okay Sam... what the hell is happenin'?"

"Jake, Dad's starting to reject the transplants. The stem cells are not regenerating the tissue as they were."

"Can you reverse it?"

"We're administering anti-rejection drugs now. I'm just not sure if they'll help."

"But he was doin' so well! What happened?"

"I can't answer that. You know I'd tell you if I could."

He looked at Jake, not wanting to continue but knowing he must disclose the EKG results. "Jake, it's not just the tissue rejection that is causing his condition."

"What do you mean?"

"He's been going so hard since the surgery he's put a great deal of stress on his heart. The EKG results show he has a serious problem. As difficult as it is for me I need to ask you this. Does Dad have his affairs in order?"

"What do you mean by that?"

"I mean has he prepared a will?"

"You haven't been around much over the past few years. Dad had his attorney put the entire operation in a non-revocable trust. He was very concerned about the place stayin' in the family. He wanted to protect us all."

Sam stared at him, not believing what he'd just heard. "You mean he included me in the trust?"

"Why hell yes, Sam. He always hoped you'd be a part of the place. You'll never know what he went through when you didn't come back to the ranch."

Samuel paused. "I didn't think it mattered to him."

"It sure as hell did matter. That's why he enjoyed Randy bein' out there helpin'. Down deep he was hopin' you'd want to be with your son and come out with 'im. He wanted us all to be together."

"And there's somethin' else you need to know. Dad stipulated that if anything happened to him, Zeb was to have a place at the ranch as long as he wanted to be there."

Sam said, "Well, after all they've been through together, who would have expected anything else? Listen, Jake. This is terribly hard for me to say, but we'd better get everyone in here. Dad could fail anytime."

They each placed calls to the family and alerted them to the pending crisis. Within three hours they were all gathered in Levi's room.

He was resting easy as he turned his head.

With a labored voice he tried to speak. "I...I want y'all to know... how proud I am of each and every one...of you. A man...couldn't ask for a finer... family. Zeb...we've had... some times. Thanks for... always stick'n by me... it's been a hell of a ride ...amigo."

With tightness in his throat Zeb moved closer. "I don't have the words, Levi. You've been the brother I never had and I love you for it."

Levi managed a weak smile as he looked at his old compadre.

Sam said, "Dad, I want you to know how brave I think you were to go out and rodeo like you did just to help pay off medical expenses and keep the ranch going. You're one hell of a man. Don't want you to worry about the ranch. My medical practice will help maintain it for everyone."

Levi looked up at Samuel and Jake tried to smile as weakness overtook him. "You boys are the best a man could ask for."

He turned his head toward the ceiling. A haze came over his eyes as he began to see an image of his lovely wife Rita standing on the porch, calling to him. Rain was pouring down, and he walked toward Rita, slipping and sliding in the heavy clay mud, rain beating down on his broad-brimmed hat. She called out to him. *"Levi, are you coming or not?"*

With a slurred, quiet voice he called back to her. "Wait, Rita. I'll be... right there." He reached out to take her hand as he slipped into eternity.

They all stood there looking at the slight smile on his face, knowing he was once again with his beloved Rita.

Sobs echoed throughout the room as they bid farewell to the old cowboy.

April rolled around, and the Blevins Ranch cowboys were gathering their cattle as it had been done for over a hundred years, a ritual that would carry on for generations to come.

Samuel sat his horse on the same knoll that Levi had been on the year before. He watched as the cowboys drove the cattle in, bunching them with those he'd gathered.

As Jake moved the cattle along, he looked towards the knoll. For a split second he visualized Levi sitting there. He shook his head, and the vision disappeared and reality set in. He urged the gray up next to his brother — stopped and watched the cattle as they slowly walked by. "It's a great feelin', isn't it Sam?"

"What do you mean?"

"I mean...it's a great feelin' knowin' we're all here together."

As they rode down to help the others drive the cattle into the branding trap, Samuel looked over at Jake. *"Yeah... it looks like we've all come full circle."*

-THE END-

About the Author

John William Mangum was born in the small northern New Mexico village of Pecos. While his father was serving in the Philippine Islands during World War II, John was relocated to Southern Arizona where he lived with his grandparents on their ranch. John's grandfather, D.C. Mangum, was instrumental in cultivating his interests in ranch life.

John spent a great deal of his youth helping friends on their ranches as well as owning cattle and horses of his own. In high school John enrolled in agriculture classes and joined the Future Farmers of America. He served as chapter president and later as an Arizona State F.F.A. Vice-President. During his high school years he participated in high school rodeo, riding bulls and team roping. He also played guitar in a small country band.

John served in the United States Army Special Forces (Airborne), better known as The Green Berets, during the Vietnam Conflict, as a demolition engineer on an "A Team". He returned home attending college, graduating from Cochise College with an Associate of Arts Degree in Business. Later he went on to obtain a Bachelor of Arts Degree from Arizona State University in History and Secondary Education.

John now lives in Southern Arizona where he writes and raises Quarter Horses. They are used for team roping, mounted shooting, barrel racing and racing. He is a licensed racehorse owner – trainer.

He is inspired by his studies in history and his many and varied life experiences. John say's "What I write is partly truth and partly fiction. The names have been changed to protect the guilty. You know who you are."

Author acknowledgments:

Jan Grams for encouragement and patience while I was writing my first novel, Full Circle.
Mark Grams for his medical assistance.
Dan Grams for design, editing, and publishing.
Bree Johnson for editing assistance.
Harvey Stanbrough for editing, encouragement and friendship.

Coming Soon:
Survivors of the Fall

Running Iron Press
P.O. Box 205
Sonoita, Arizona 85637

(520) 604-0114
info@runningironpress.com